SOULLESS

PALMETTO

P U B L I S H I N G
Charleston, SC
www.PalmettoPublishing.com

Hardcover ISBN: 979-8-8229-3024-7
Paperback ISBN: 979-8-8229-3025-4

SOULLESS

Fatoumata Nabie Fofana

Dedication

To the legacy of my rare Momma, Fanta Konneh.
I miss you, but I know you are happy, and without pain in heaven.
1959 - 2019

PROLOGUE

Life outside of our triangular condominium buzzed with pleasurable energy. This unsettled my dad, who worked his hardest to shield me from worldly things. Uncompromising in his religious belief, Papa would, from time to time, thoroughly scan every inch of my matchbox-sized bedroom, looking for anything suspicious.

He read the Qur'an in Arabic and diligently performed the five daily prayers. Papa made countless charitable donations, fasted all thirty days of the Holy Month of Ramadan, and was mindful of his utterances. In his quest to keep me sanctified, Papa became overly protective. He had rules for whom I could see, and what I could say and do.

At home, I was a second-class citizen. Papa often frowned at me for what he considered "*wasting*" my life on things that were "*unworthy*" of my "*hereafter*".

"The life of this *Dunya* is but a comfort of illusion" was his favorite line. "Be mindful of your duty towards the womb that bore you and do as I say," he would add.

Momma wouldn't dare interfere. I knew she never approved of Papa's somewhat difficult relationship with me. During those days, women were groomed and coached to be submissive, including adhering to their husbands' decisions, regardless of whether they (wives) disliked them.

The truth is, like everything else around me, I could tell that our world was in a downward spiral. Our days were sliced to twelve hours instead of twenty-four; our lives ended fast. Death was no longer a thing for the old—young folks were taking the lead. Sickness was no longer a passage to death. Children, young adults, and babies were suddenly departing our world.

It was clear that soon, we would all face a Mighty Being for a final judgment to determine whether we would be spending eternity in *Al Jannat* or *Jahim*. Until then, we all assumed that the time of doomsday was concealed from humankind. Some even thought it was still a million years out while others believed it was a fairytale. In all the concerns over our world coming to an end, one doomsday scenario that stood out for me was the recurrence of pre-historic events, such as widespread incest, rivers morphing into stagnant streams of blood, newborns having adult-like features, rapid deaths, among many others. A sudden outbreak of an infectious, incurable disease claimed millions of lives worldwide. Herbalists far and near grappled with tracing the roots of this disease and its cure. The disease's ability to kill half a million people in a split second was deeply terrifying. More importantly, its shapeshifting ability quickly dashed any hope for an anti-*baramorsama* arsenal.

There was a year when folks weaved in and out of graveyards like ants in an anthill. Cemeteries across the countryside and city were overcrowded, and holes were dug into existing graves to accommodate newcomers. Grave cleaning and maintenance soon became a thing—it was the only way to safeguard your beloved's new haven from being broken into, all in the name of creating more rooms for newly dead bodies.

That year, Christian and Muslim bodies shared the same cemeteries. Until then, burying Muslims and non-Muslims in mixed cemeteries was inappropriate. Islam strictly forbade it. There were specific Islamic teachings regarding washing, enshrouding, burying the dead, grave visitation, and praying for the dead.

Disregard for longstanding traditional practices, coupled with the disappearance of age-old cultural and religious beliefs, was widespread. Male chauvinism was under attack from all sides. A previous religious taboo—interfaith marriages between Muslims and non-Muslims—was suddenly a mainstay. Eating with the left hand was no longer frowned upon. These rapid changes only fueled the anxiety that our world was fast approaching its end.

* * *

Though these happenings equally disrupted my family traditions, I still wasn't sure how or when our world would come crashing down, and this had me thinking twice about my dad's guidance.

I assumed his constant scolding was his way of getting me disinterested in life. *After all, what's the essence of living when you must abstain from life's joyful experiences?* I wondered. I was young, ambitious, fearless, and full of adventures. Yet I was a geeky girl in town, had very few friends, and lived a severely controlled life within the walls of our condo. I wished so much to give in to my greedy, perhaps clueless desire to take on the world, and I wanted to do that without holding my breath or pacifying my surging lungs. But then again, Papa invested a hefty portion of his time into monitoring my movements, utterances, and appearance. He scrutinized every word I uttered for religious suitability or social correctness. I was swiftly growled at for slight '*infractions*' as wearing a pair of high-waisted jeans and cropped tops; these were considered unfit for me. "You are a girl," Papa was quick to point out.

"Pants are for boys," my insanely snoopy paternal aunt would shout, alarming the entire neighborhood of a heinous crime. Tantie Mamièn knew how to ignite tension between Papa and me. "As a girl, your right fit is modest wear. How about a nice abaya or kimono, or even a cardigan? They do a wonderful job of veiling your body," she would go on. "Don't you see how beautiful your peers look wearing such outfits? Their hassle-free life should inspire you," she would yell, intentionally seeking Papa's attention. "You are an embarrassment to this family…just like your mom," she would add, pausing for Papa's reaction. And if he said nothing, she would say, "You should never expose parts of your body that aren't meant for the public's eye." She'd say this through a wry smile. And if she truly meant to get Papa riled, she would add, "Your dress code is your brand; it tells a lot about who you are and affects how people perceive and treat you. Modesty, combined with morality, defines womanhood." This statement would send Papa into a tailspin. He would shoot me his signature supervillain look that always startled me and made me scurry through the tiny door that led into my bedroom.

That was the least you could expect of Tantie Mamièn. She was uber manipulative, the ultimate peace spoiler, and the truest example of a havoc-monger. The worst part? She was a deep source of psychological torment for girls in my family. It took us a long time to figure out that Tantie Mamièn was abusing us. And even then, I questioned my judgment and sanity. That's how damaging her impact was.

Deep down, I knew I wasn't crazy, not making things up about her. Neither was I being a crybaby. Her passive-aggressive warfare had me confused! Her secret weapon? Veiled insults. To top it off, Tantie Mamièn had zero interest in or empathy for anyone but herself. And guess what? She always got away with her narcissistic actions.

* * *

Everything about Tantie Mamièn was sinister save her dazzling beauty. There was nothing average about her. Her perfectly polished teeth, sharply cut neck-length hair, and unnaturally golden skin had everyone gasping. She had plump, naturally black lips and gums, which were outstanding, especially since every woman in my family had to endure the pain of tattooing their lips and gums for that seductive, signature smile.

Inspired by an ancient tradition, tattooed black gums and lips were a big thing of beauty in my family; it was an obsession. Every girl underwent the procedure, which was never performed out of a parlor but in the backyard of Tantie Masiagbè's mud hut. She was the family's lone gum and lip tattoo artist. She had the hottest, sexiest pout in the history of lips in my family.

She was medium height with silk skin that looked nothing less than dashing pearls. Her orange hair was enticing, but more importantly, her enviable lips turned heads.

"Listen, tattooed gums and white teeth are the perfect pair," she would tell me, trying to lure me into becoming a customer. "They are enticing." If I remained unbothered, she would add, "There's zero room for bloodshot gums in this family."

"Is that a threat?"

"I don't care what it is, but understand that your gums must be as dark as a moonless night to attract potential suitors," she would add, concluding that "a beautiful, stainless smile attracts men."

"Must it always be about impressing men? Men, men… it's always about men. Smh…"

"Why are you so stubborn? If your father isn't careful, you will bring great shame to this family…foolish girl."

* * *

Tantie Masiagbè didn't perform her art for the money but for the love of it. She charged roughly one dollar per procedure and administered the tattoo using a black powdered mixture from burning shea butter blended with palm oil. During those days, we used palm oil to cook most meals. Vegetable oil was never a thing. No wonder it was labeled *tiatoulou*. It was unattractive and quickly stained the appearance of a sumptuous stew with its dull, dusty look. We weren't interested in painting a fish or okra stew with tomato paste either. Palm oil did the job so effortlessly.

Tantie Masiagbè's clients rested their heads on her lap while she generously applied the black powder to their gums before poking them with a bundle of eighty needles. She applied seven to eight black powder layers and subsequently blended each layer into the gums with the needles, causing them to become dyed black. Clients were prohibited from crying or using gestures indicating they were being tortured. Doing so was a display of weakness, which was an unacceptable taboo. In those days, women and girls were trained to swallow their pain, including during childbirth.

*   *   *

Luckily for Tantie Mamièn, she never had to endure this gruesome act. She was the family's most beautiful woman, nevertheless. Her eye-catching, heart-shaped lips were naturally coated in black; her lusciously dark gums blessed her with the perfect smile. She often wore hooded attires to partially cover her almond-shaped eyes, clad so dangerously underneath puffs of seductive smokey lashes. Turtle-necked outfits were her favorite weekend styles. I always believed her astonishing beauty was a cover-up for her selfish actions.

Regardless, Tantie Mamièn's ultimate goal was to see me veiled from head to toe, which would have been great if the decision to do that had been truly mine. I didn't want to wear a hijab because I was forced to or to please others. Doing so would have been fueled by falsehood, which, I knew, often ended with revulsion. I wanted that decision to originate from my heart.

I staged silent protests as the sharp scolding intensified. I shielded my activities, reducing the chance of attracting too much attention or causing an unnecessary stir. By then, Papa's subtle threats of forcing me into an arranged marriage were ferocious.

*   *   *

We ate with our bare hands, together, from an oversized, plastic pan. Spoons were reserved for hot brews such as tea or coffee. Dinner was primarily our dietary staple—steamed swamp rice with meat broth. At the time, most people preferred parboiled swamp rice because of its ease on the stomach. White rice was never a favorite due to its starchy nature and associated glucose stigma. We cooked three times a day, beginning with *Lafidi*, our usual breakfast dish—plain rice mixed with okra paste and perfect seasoning. We ate *Lafidi* seven days a week. The sharp taste of bitter balls mixed with *soumbarafeen* smashed our taste buds to perfection. Cooking *Lafidi* was easy:

- Slice the okra and bitter balls and place them in boiling water.
- After they've boiled for fifteen minutes, add the rice.
- As the rice steams, add salt, spices, powdered fish, and *soumbarafeen*.
- Be sure the water is completely dry before fishing for bitter balls and okra.
- Manually blend the okra and bitter balls, then mix the paste with the rice to give it a slippery, slightly bitter taste. The other ingredients are mixed in later to create the perfect *Lafidi* served with fresh palm oil.

For lunch, we ate Tô, a dish made from powdered cassava mixed with corn porridge and served with okra soup. Personally, I loved Tô. My taste buds were captivated by its subtle yet punchy taste every time I had it. Dinner consisted of steamed rice served with either *nanjee* or *tiajee*.

* * *

My job was to clean up our dining spot. Mama hated seeing dirty dishes lingering until the next morning. I manually washed and dried all the dishes in the backyard. Then, I would sweep the front porch with a broom made of small palm straws. While I swept one night, I overheard Papa tell Mama, "My uncle's son has expressed interest in your daughter. I think he would be a good match."

"I'm sorry to interrupt, but aren't we rushing this?" responded Momma.

"I'm worried about your daughter. Her thirst for this *Dunya* is wilder than ever. I will be at peace knowing she is married."

Suddenly, I became nauseous and shivered. Back then, teenage marriage was popular even though it was frowned upon in many parts of my community. For most parents, child brides were a source of pride and honor for their families. Whenever a girl saw her first menstruation, she was next in line to get married. Most parents feared that an unwanted pregnancy would damage their family's honor. As a result, they worked 24/7 to get their daughters married as early as possible.

* * *

From then on, I wore floor-length gowns as coverups for my hot pants or booty shorts and cropped tops while leaving or returning home. I avoided places frequented by relatives, never wanting them to discover my new two-phased lifestyle: fully-veiled at home but fully exposed to the world outside of our condo.

At home, my hair was a thing of privacy. I listened to Quranic content only. My bed soon became a field of sticky notes with Quranic quotes and inspirations. *Ayat Kursi* was now my slogan. In short, my life within our condo was suddenly focused on my hereafter in order to soften Papa's stance. The idea of an arranged marriage scared me. I had big dreams, but I was worried Papa would crush them.

My disdainful acts would eventually come to haunt me, and I wished I had heeded Papa's instructions sooner rather than later.

CONTENTS

PART ONE
Fear of the Unknown

In a world nearing extinction, my dad spent plenty of time reminding me of life's brevity. Our increasingly corrupted moral values only pointed to the final destruction of humanity—the day when the Almighty would examine our acts and intentions for moral suitability. Of course, we were never to live on Earth for eternity, but we were equally unprepared for the speed with which doomsday was headed our way. Papa would say, "Life is as brief as operating a souk. It doesn't matter how long your hours of operations are or how busy you are with meeting the competing needs and demands of clients; there comes the point when everything STOPS." The point being that, no matter what, a souk eventually shuts its doors. And so did life. The only difference was that a bazaar's closing time was known, while life's endpoint was unknown.

Life, at the time, was temporary, yet, its expiration was timeless, very fluid. Papa always wanted me to be wary and heedful of this volatility of life's ultimate end throughout my journey of existence. He never failed to raise the red flag whenever I was *suspected* of falling even so slightly for the temptations of this worldly life: "It's not as if you have all the time in this

Dunya. The sad part is that He never tells you how much time you have to live. You could die in a few decades or in an hour. Death is life's definitive surprise. So, make every second count by living righteously."

I get it, but most of my peers at the time lacked spiritual influence. They had compromised morals, lacked intimacy with their Maker, and reluctantly gave up what society considered "*sinful*" acts, such as partying, dating, dancing, or singing. They were friends of the world and fans of worldly things. They were passionate lovers of showbiz. Though some were never allowed to go clubbing, they created weekly nightclubs in their bedrooms. MoaKula and MoaMuyan, my closest friends, knew nearly every song's lyrics well before it was released. Like them, I too wanted to wear massive wigs and large hoop earrings. I wanted to sport my cute legs in hot pants and my flat tummy in crop tops. I wanted to explore the various nightclubs that lined La Rue Princesse. I wanted to have a boyfriend too! Nevertheless, Papa's stiff reminders were hard to ignore. "Be aware that only your deeds will follow you into your grave, not your fancy, empty, fleshly life. And you better ensure that your good deeds outweigh the other," he would say.

Death, as we knew it, was an angry entity, and our fancy world was bound to eventually surrender to its inescapable jaws—though not a single soul knew the exact date or time of this imminent doom. Amid this uncertainty, Papa heightened his nagging fear. He pushed me to live a modest life built on the five pillars of Islam: the profession of faith (the *shahada*), praying five times a day, fasting for thirty days during the month of Ramadan, providing for the needy (*zakat*), and performing the Hajj (pilgrimage). Papa believed modesty was about cutting ties with this world's fantasy. It meant understanding my calling and living a life that would pave my way to heaven—wherever that is—someday.

* * *

It angered me that Papa was anxious about the afterlife when doomsday remained unknown. News of a relative's death weighed heavily on him as he aged. He was afraid of dying, yet he spent his entire life preparing for the hereafter. Our world was shrinking, reinforcing the jolt that he would join our forefathers someday. I allowed him to fret, while longing for a chance to exploit the joy of living. My bucket list was dripping with passion. I wanted to be a super catwalker and a print model without equal. Oh yes, I wanted to wear bikinis on stage for the world to see what a beautiful angel I was. I was obsessed with fashion and dreamed of living it, but I had kept it secret from everyone, including myself. I dreamed of meeting great folks like Samori Toure, Shaka Zulu, Thomas Sankara, Nelson Mandela, and Oprah. I desired to visit fancy places like Santorini, Greece; Venice, Italy; Paris, France; Baku, Azerbaijan; and Abu Dhabi.

As a teenager, my worldview took on a more defined structure. Instead of worrying too much about the doomsday scenario, I loosened up to exploit the invaluable gift of living, at least until death's inevitable claws devoured me. Such a tête-à-tête was destined anyway. I no longer desired to be enslaved by it. I wanted to be free, breaking up with my two-phased lifestyle. I was hungry to unleash my overdue, blossoming desire to taste every aspect of life. I wanted to do everything Papa considered "*worldly*" or "*sinful.*"

Every time he brought up his doomsday topic, I did not sense fear or self-pity; only resentment crept up on my face. I avoided everyone attempting to lure me into living in fear of the unknown. There was much more to live for, explore, discover, and learn. I didn't see the point in burying these opportunities because Papa was so afraid of what he knew not.

Granted. Nothing lasted forever. I was acutely aware that every soul would taste the sting of death, but I also knew that no soul would die unless He had willed it. I was aware that every soul would be paid on the day of resurrection only that which they had fairly earned. I also knew that evildoers would have no helper on That Day and that choosing the devil for a patron was a mortal's greatest mistake. All that said, I had a life to live and was guided by the idea that death only targeted older people. I didn't care if there was no cure for aging or that not everyone was blessed to experience aging. Some folks died very young; some died as infants.

In short, I refused to allow this fear of uncertainty to control me. I went about my daily life freely until June 10, 2019, when a mixture of grief and terror sliced my heart open. I was forced to reevaluate my relationship with life.

PART TWO

The Journey

One minute, I was attending school because Momma succeeded in convincing Papa to let me. The next minute, I was out because Papa was back to his belief that school was "*worldly*." Momma's unwavering determination enabled me to finish high school, even though it took me several years longer than I expected. The same thing happened when I chose a career path Papa considered "*sinister.*" I was deeply passionate about the film industry as a child. It was my dream to direct and produce films of all genres. Visual arts inspired me to create cartoon characters and stories that taught children to do good deeds. The idea didn't appeal to Papa because it involved mingling with "too many people."

Upon graduating from high school, I began working for a local multimedia firm as a writer. The nature of this job troubled Papa. His fear this time? I would be distracted. Momma spent several months convincing him to allow me to cultivate my passion. I served in various editorial roles, including becoming the first female content editor of a major magazine in my ancestral hometown. Merrivylle's leading independent publishing house,

MirrorIt, produced and circulated one hundred fifty thousand magazines daily.

That was my life until I landed an international fellowship to pursue my studies overseas, in a country called *Saboudou*.

* * *

Mama rallied chief imams across the seven villages and towns to convince Papa to let me go. Having dropped out of ninth grade, Momma understood the importance of education and believed it should be accessible to all. Momma was pulled out of school and given to a man she barely knew, but with whom she spent the rest of her life. In spite of her limited education, she was determined to see me flourish as a woman on my own. In contrast, Papa was raised culturally and never exposed to secular education. He was a staunch traditionalist.

At one of the meetings between Papa and the imams, Momma got a chance to speak. In her words, "Education helps girls to make sound decisions, hold their families together, and support and contribute to societal growth and development." She said, "Take me as an example; my small education allows me to read and write your letters. Additionally, my business strategies differ greatly from my peers. I have opened many stalls and vending stations in the various towns and villages. The majority of my friends sell only to feed their families. From *hand-to-mouth* is what they call it. I do that..., but I also save some money to invest in other sectors of our dormant economy. That's how I open a new stall every other month... education helps you make sound decisions and approach life differently."

She continued, "We have been blessed with a wondrous child. Please don't punish her because of her gender."

"Why would you say that?" Papa interrupted.

"It's only because she's a girl that you are hard on her. Why should her gender be used to limit her access to education, especially higher education?

This is a good decision…not just for her, but for this entire family and community." Momma had no fear; she believed I could be faithful to my religious doctrine and follow my passions at the same time. Papa agreed eventually. I was an emotional wreck, happy to be studying abroad, but reluctant to be separated from Momma, my one and only hero. I can't describe how special our mother-daughter bond was.

It was finally departure day. I gathered my clothes and a few belongings in a shabby suitcase that had collected dust in our attic. Tantie Mamièn didn't like the valise either.

"I'd like a Gucci suitcase. Not *that thing*."

"You don't have to be so mean," I said, searching Momma's face for a reaction, and *there* was her famous *let-it-go* look. She was good at communicating with her eyes. She was a woman of few words. A doer, not a talker.

A wild spender and never satisfied with brandless items, Tantie Mamièn had a tremendous taste for pricey things. That's why she was divorced so many times—it had to be Gucci, Versace, Louis Vuitton, Chanel, or Coach. Her fourth husband, Morrigbè, lasted a year and was ready to end it, as had his predecessors. During a family meeting convened to mend their deeply fractured marriage, he stated, "I sleep with money in my underpants. She steals my money and wastes it! She stole $500 from my shirt last week and spent it immediately. My in-laws, consider this marriage over if Mamièn fails to return those funds within three days."

* * *

Life in *Saboudou*, a faraway land, was bizarre. It wasn't what I expected. An unforgiving sense of hopelessness was now my staple. And no, I wasn't homesick, even though not having Momma's physical love around was a bit of a torment. Nothing else seemed to hold in this new land. *Saboudou* was a fancy land predominantly inhabited by members of the Kônô tribe. The Kônôs were famed for their sparkly, gemlike skyscrapers lining every city's central business district. These eye-popping structures were unique to *Saboudou*, and visitors from far and near flocked in and out to catch a glimpse and get a firsthand feel of what it was like to spend a day in the land of limitless opportunities—hence, its name *Saboudou*.

Regardless, it never dawned on me that moving to *Saboudou* would crush my dream of becoming a first-rate communications tycoon. It never occurred to me that those little things I had in life—my job, the love of my mom, siblings, and community—were priceless gifts until I lost them all in this strange land. It felt like I had just been born. I even missed Papa.

My skills honed over the years were suddenly useless. I lost every chance of furthering my career. Every journalism job I applied for returned with a rejection letter until I was drowning in rejection letters from companies around the country. Even though I was qualified for most of the openings I applied for, I was rejected. This hurt so much; I felt let down, which made it harder to cope.

I had to start life afresh. I felt out of place in this new land. My education was trashed, my skin color was an issue, my accent was a problem, and my name - Manatou Lahai - raised red flags. My ancestral hometown, Merrivylle, was branded as a place infested with death, destruction, and disease. A notion like this fueled resentment toward me, shattering the glitz and glamour I imagined this faraway land to have. I was forced to outwork and outdo myself just to fit in, even a high school dropout felt superior to me. Whether thrown in my face directly or subtly, racism constantly confronted me:

- An employee at a shoe store followed me around because I matched the profile of a shoplifter.
- My bosses considered my accent to be an indication of inadequacy, leading to derogatory and demeaning comments.

- I had to consistently outdo myself to demonstrate my authenticity because the foundation of my education was a place "overwhelmed by wars, diseases, genocides, and extreme famine."

* * *

"Is your new chair comfortable?"

"Yes. Thank you," I said.

"I'm glad you do because your previous chair was very hard on your butt," Mark said.

"Excuse me!" I said, tears gathering in both eyes. I felt belittled in front of my coworkers.

Mark continued adamantly, "It's the truth. In addition to being too skinny, your butts have very thin flesh. A cushioned chair would be more comfortable for you."

It was my first encounter with emotional abuse at work, and what made it remarkable was that it was from an EMPLOYER! What was my reaction? You might ask, "didn't you walk out and sue him?" I wish it was that simple. I had just started this job, was new to this country, had no idea where I was headed, and had no idea how the [legal] system worked. Surviving was all I could think about.

* * *

An inner voice said, "Take a deep breath. Take a deep breath. Certainly, he does not respect human dignity. You should quit." Another voice added, "That's a risky move. It means returning to the job market, which is saturated at the moment. It's not worth the risk. Rent and food cost money. Also, don't forget how much Momma relies on you financially. Manatou, you have a huge responsibility on your shoulders."

"I agree," said a tiny voice. "This is part of what our people back home call "*toungban*"…journeying to unknown places comes with unexpected

9

consequences, unexpected prices to pay. You must go through these struggles today to have a story to inspire someone with tomorrow."

"Let it go and get back to work," concluded all three voices. I had just started my second week at the company. My job was to resurrect a dead natural hair brand, which involved hiring and training three telemarketers, three sales agents, and a receptionist. Mark was my first employer in *Saboudou*. He owned a marketing company in a vibrant city on the East Coast. I was a bachelor's degree candidate, an experienced journalist, and a brand marketer with excellent writing, editing, and management skills. In addition, I spoke multiple languages (Français, Bambara, Koniaké, Twi, Fula, Soso, and more), which were the same languages spoken by the product's target consumers.

Mark wrote in the offer letter, "I will start you at twelve dollars an hour."

"Considering my experience and other skills, I will take fifteen dollars."

"I don't mind. Because you are also licensed in health, life, and casualty insurance, I will pay you twelve dollars per hour and purchase employee policies from you. In addition to the remaining three dollars, you will earn more in commission." I found that feasible, only to discover that Mark already had contracts with external agents that would only renew after ten years.

* * *

After all that, Mark "*modernized*" my name because "Manatou Lahai" came across as too primitive. "I massaged it a little bit. Customers will have difficulty pronouncing 'Manatou Lahai'. It's a little rough on the tongue. I prefer 'Matou Lahai'."

"Without my consent? Do you really think you can get away with this? Please use my REAL name or remove my face from your magazine."

"Then what? Over a million copies are in circulation! Are you kidding me?"

Shivering, I said, "You did not inform me of a name change when you asked me to attend the cover shoot. This is a complete violation of my rights."

"You are now the face of a major brand. It's great publicity for you."

As he walked away, he said, "Look on the bright side."

In the evening, I telephoned a maternal aunt living nearby. *Saboudou* had been her home for over ten years. "My dear, that's our life in this country. You now understand why we get offended when people back home complain that we send them 'just fifty dollars' as a stipend. We SUFFER a lot in this country! There may not always be a physical component. It can be emotional...like what your employer is doing to you. You're being abused, but what can you do? There is nothing! Don't even think about taking legal action because you can't afford it!" explained Tantie Ramatta.

"Act as though nothing has happened. You will be out of there one day."

"Ok. Thanks, Tantie."

"Good night, my dear."

"Good night, Tantie.

* * *

I resigned from Mark's Saint Media and became a style blogger at Jolieden Ya Closet, but I still faced similar biases. Thank goodness none of the discrimination or negativity projected outwardly on my ancestral hometown could derail me or dissuade me from my Merrivylle pride. They prepared me for a rather rough journey in this strange land.

I took a leave of absence from work to concentrate on my studies a few years later. In order to cement my authenticity among coworkers and managers, I needed a third or fourth academic layer. I assumed that a graduate degree from an Ivy League school would enhance my brand and make me more marketable. After a job search that stretched on forever, I was left with an endless loop of frustration. The rejection notices this time were punchier.

* * *

As my job search woes worsened, I attended numerous trainings and consulted hundreds of career coaches. Returning to school to improve my academic and professional skills was now my greatest mistake. As I entered my second year of joblessness, I redirected my efforts toward finding a job in direct marketing, eventually landing a part-time position at *The Crown* fashion magazine. I worked as an advertising specialist, an entry-level position far below my professional and academic levels. Having to accept a professional demotion was the least of my worries at the time. What was my real fear? Eroding skills. My value on the labor market was at risk after a 24-month pause. My effectiveness in a new role could be threatened by any lingering damage to my skills.

Moreover, I was sickened by the constant feeling that I was a burden on my parents. My scholarship stipend and paycheck had both stopped. I received rent and food money from Merrivylle, and Federal Financial Aid paid for my education. In a perfect world, I would have provided for my family back home. Exactly why? As compared to Merrivylle's salary standards, I was now living abroad and earning a "decent" income.

Reestablishing myself was difficult and I was bullied by relatives. I was asked daily, "Who defaults on their duty to their family?"

"You owe it to them. So, get up and get out!" Uncle O. would scream.

I got it, but was it really that simple? I submitted twenty satisfactory job applications per day…and by satisfactory, I mean preparing professional cover letters per application, ensuring they aligned well with each job's description; completing application booklets sometimes comprising fifty discriminatory questions; responding to other nonapplication-related questions to please HR personnel; completing discriminatory job-related surveys that compelled you to reveal your gender, religion, and race; investing thirty to forty minutes in weird personality tests that never reflected who you truly were but what HR personnel believed defined you.

I attended job fairs and filled out applications from various companies. My search also involved visiting hundreds of marketing companies' websites. I spent time flagging myself on Indeed.com, LinkedIn, CareerBuilder, and so on. Although I, my siblings, and my parents all needed money, my efforts yielded nothing. The thought of my peers advancing in life drowned me in self-pity. I avoided people, especially relatives. I always had an excuse not to attend a family function. I didn't want anyone asking me, "Any luck yet?" I created a private zone belonging to me and my loneliness. Nevertheless, I didn't stop knocking.

* * *

It was my daring spirit that earned me a position at Notre Dame. My company's corporate office was nestled in Cherry City, a vibrant city in *Saboudou*. My first months were spent canvassing on major streets, in crowded malls, and at major outreach events. Eight months later, my role was modified. Now I was anchored on the sixteenth floor of the *Lagaré* Building in the city's central business district. I was responsible for maintaining the company's website and social media accounts. I developed, designed, and updated these platforms with compelling, engaging content to drive online traffic.

In addition, I handled all brand marketing initiatives, including press releases published in the *CherriBiz Mag*, sales scripts for the marketing and customer service teams, flyers, how-to guides, brochures, and magazine ads. *CherriBiz Mag* was published monthly, distributed through direct mail nationwide, and targeted a half-million circulation.

When momma heard this news, she was beyond thrilled. "This is just the beginning," she said during a WhatsApp conversation. As we talked, I mentioned my subtle longing to see her. I asked her how she was doing. Everything was fine, she assured me.

Two years later, I joined *Les Médiateurs*, an international nonprofit organization, as a writer and web content editor. I developed and directed major editorial projects, such as the organization's high-performing *Dive Talk* platform. This interactive podcast accepted, screened, edited, and broadcasted scholarly articles. Two years later, I joined *InterCome* as a private tutor, focusing on relationship-building. I used active listening and effective communication to convert one-time clients into returning patrons of our Strawberry Gift Cards and MyStraw products.

I joined the city government a year later as a diplo data specialist (DDS), overseeing and coordinating the Law Depot's charging unit. This role entailed interfacing with foreign mission staff, senior national security officers, court clerks, detectives, the press, and the public. It allowed me to apply my years of experience as a skilled content developer and strategist to enhance the Law Depot's marketing and communications efforts.

On my end, everything seemed to be moving more quickly. I was opening more and more doors. Nonetheless, in Merrivylle, my ancestral hometown, Momma was grappling with her off-and-on health issues.

PART THREE

The Power of Hope

Momma's condition was deteriorating fast. She had lost significant weight and was now confined to her bedroom after several unsuccessful foot surgeries. She required 24/7 care; her medical needs and bills soared. My earnings at the time were enough to ensure that she received quick and quality care. Yet the pain I endured whenever Momma underwent a routine health crisis was indescribable. I cried and prayed, but Momma would never walk or leave her bedroom again.

I longed and prayed for the Almighty to transfer her poor health onto me and restore her inner peace and freedom. Unlike me, Momma remained cheerful, prayerful, and hopeful throughout her sickness. She was strong and consoling, urging me to be tough, not for her but for myself. If anything, I admired her optimism and learned a lot from how she handled her illness: her smiles never faded. She ignored her worsening condition, focusing solely on what made her happy. Momma was never depressed by her inability to do the things that had previously been a significant part of her life: seeing new buds, admiring the birds, feeling fresh leaves, and seeing cattle and chickens. Sometimes she went into a coma for days but bounced right back.

She recovered from a major health crisis a week before June 10, 2019, after passing out while performing the congregational prayer during Eid-Al-Fitr. This development impaired our ability to uphold our family's ingrained Eid tradition that year.

Eid-Al-Fitr is the first day of the month immediately preceding Ramadan. It is the day Muslims celebrate the end of fasting. Immediately after sunset on the 29th day of Ramadan, Muslim scholars search for the crescent. If sighted, it is the first day of the new month—marking the beginning of Eid festivities. Muslims fast on the thirtieth day of Ramadan if the crescent isn't sighted. On Eid day, they gather in larger facilities, such as soccer fields, large playgrounds, or community centers for the Eid prayer, led by an imam (a Muslim prayer leader).

* * *

As a Muslim family, Eid-Al-Fitr was a joyous day for us. After observing thirty days of fasting and praying for Allah's blessings, compassion, and enlightenment, we enjoyed the day marking the end of the holiest and purest of all months—Ramadan. Our Eid tradition was defined by family, fashion, and food. Eid was a chance to cherish the things our *family* valued the most, such as our culture. Our outfits were handmade, one-of-a-kind haute *fashion*, and the different *foods* we prepared for this special occasion directly reflected our tradition in action.

That year, I ordered a handcrafted, custom-made kimono for Eid. It was absolutely stunning. The length was perfect, the V-neck was sassy, and the puffy sleeves completed this adorable outfit. There was something aristocratic about the color *blue* in the fabric. It was enticing and highlighted the golden flowers in the material's heart perfectly. Until then, yellow was my favorite color. It was my belief that we all needed the warmth of sunlight to glow in the perfect way. However, the fierceness of blue in this formidable hibiscus fabric shook me out of my color selection. So, I added royal blue to my list, which was a great mix.

*   *   *

I was fashion-obsessed and couldn't wait to wear my stylish dress and feel like a fairytale princess waiting to meet her prince charming. I was fascinated by all things Merrivylle, the land of my forefathers, despite moving to *Saboudou*.

*   *   *

My ancestral home was a tiny island state along the northern cape of *Farafina*, one of the poorest on the continent, with a GDP per capita of $400. Ninety percent of the country's population survived on blended farming—subsistence and cash crop—and inhabited the hinterlands. About ten percent of the population survived on trans-state trades of traditional batik and wax fabrics, cattle, pure gold, silver dust, uncut gems of incredible proportions, salt, and kola nuts.

The country's economy was dominated by agriculture; it thrived from October through January when cashew farmers harvested, dried, and shipped their raw produce to international processors before it was sold to consumers globally. Thanks to its unyielding cocoa farmers, Merrivylle became the world's largest producer and exporter of raw cocoa beans. It was the darling of the world's chocolate lovers. The country also had abundant deposits of crude oil along its coast. And while 90 percent of the population lived far beneath the economy's lowest ebb, only 2 percent had access to a bank and health insurance. Life insurance was utterly nonexistent. It was considered a sinister business or act and was punishable by long prison terms. Religion, blended with unaltered traditional cultures, forbade this type of insurance in its entirety.

*   *   *

While the lack of life insurance was never a big deal for many, its absence birthed serious consequences that most families couldn't bear. Whenever a family's main income earner died, and the paycheck stopped coming in, the survivors stressed about paying the burial costs and settling any debts the deceased may have had. For the most part, these expenses were paid out-of-pocket, which wasn't always easy for the bulk of the population. Keep in mind that folks could barely afford to feed themselves. If this were your case, you would rely on external family members' and neighbors' contributions to bury your loved ones while stressing about what to eat and how to pay your rent and utility bills. It was an unnecessary burden to shoulder.

Telecommunications almost did not exist in Merrivylle. Folks with conventional landline phones anchored in dust-covered corners of their homes were the shakers and movers of our society—ethically undisciplined politicians or political thieves made up the bulk of this group.

However, Merrivylle had its unique, hard-to-ignore natural attraction. It was heaven on earth. The scenery was mind-blowing. Its five hundred plus dialects, traditions, cultures, historical sites, drinks, and native foods made it an irresistible destination for tourists.

Merrivylle's scenic beauty impressed travelers. There was a shimmering lake, known to locals as *The Glow*, nestled among lush mountains, surrounded by treeless, flat land. The country was renowned for its unbending kwanza cherry, northern red, and baby giant arborvitae trees that whispered in soothing winds. During the harmattan season, the blossoming kwanza cherry trees would smile with pinkish blooms, backed by magenta rays from the northern trees in between the dark-green baby giant arborvitae trees. All of these things made Merrivylle look like a beautifully decorated *Koniaka* bride, ready to start her happily ever after.

I was so proud of this wonderful paradise on earth. I grew up there, and it remained a crucial part of my childhood. My hometown was *N'dianamösso*, located on the country's west coast. The town was tiny but densely populated.

Most of its inhabitants lived in not-so-luxurious condominiums. My family lived in one of the brick-powered homes in *N'dianamösso* when I was a child. In our twenty-story building, my parents' condo occupied the eleventh floor, giving me a wonderful view of the *Badénya* Mountains and the rolling *Signônya* Hills. The *Badénya* Mountains towered over the city, watching its inhabitants relentlessly. There was peace and beauty in my hometown.

For Eid that year, Samira, my older sister, made me a pantsuit that was groundbreaking. From the perplexing designs and techniques to the gorgeous styles they were stitched into, Merrivylle prints were a slice of heaven…and paradise lived on earth in Merrivylle. I had two spectacular outfits to wear, but Eid that year changed our lives forever.

* * *

Racing heart. Soaring anxiety. There were countless mishaps that marred my day, all indicative of the gloomy clouds heading my way. Taking a step aside, I dialed Samira's number.

"How is Momma doing?"

"She is not feeling well. At the prayer today, she passed out and was rushed to the hospital."

"Just like that?"

"Yes. Very strange."

"And you said she passed out?"

"Yes. She was placed on oxygen."

I waded in waves of shock and daze as Samira spoke. Sweat drenched my palms. The droplets from my fingers soaked the front of my outfit as I held the phone to my ear. If not for divine intervention, I would have peed myself. I trembled, my hair strands reached for the stars, and tears ran down my cheeks. My flesh, organs, and soul were all compromised. Soulless, I felt.

"We are home now. She spent four hours in the hospital."

"Please give her the phone." I can still recall the sweetness of Momma's voice as we talked that afternoon.

"I'm fine. Don't let this ruin your day. It's a special day."

"Well, so much for celebration," I mused.

"How can I when you are lying in bed, battling this sickness again?"

"I made it to the prayer, and we should all be thankful for that," Momma said, joyfully. "My image was captured by angels monitoring congregational prayers around the globe. That's a priceless blessing, isn't it? In a religious sense, I feel fulfilled. Today is the happiest day of my life," she said, working miracles in every fiber of my being.

Momma was right. Eid-Al-Fitr didn't only signify the *breaking of fast*. After fasting on food and drinks from sunrise to sunset for thirty days, believers assembled for a unique, obligatory prayer on the morning of Eid. During this prayer, the seven heavens were torn apart, and angels descended to take headcounts of every soul at every prayer ground around the world. On that day, Momma was indeed counted among the blessed.

She was unable to fast during Ramadan due to her medical condition. She took a million pills throughout the day. In spite of this, she faithfully paid zakat and performed special prayers, such as praying during the night when the world was fast asleep. Her desire to be intimate with her Creator motivated her to do more charitable deeds and perform salat religiously. Little did we know that our rare Momma was on her way to ultimate rest.

* * *

The shortness of breath lingered. For an entire week, Momma went in and out of the hospital. It would leave her for a while but then return with much severity. Through it all, she sounded very alert. She would chat with me on WhatsApp calls at length. Though we tried to give hope a chance, we knew deep within us that she wasn't doing well. This time, everything about her was very different. Unlike the significant life-threatening health crises she was accustomed to, this stage of her deteriorating health was rather asymptomatic for the first few days, until she began dozing off very frequently. She would be talking to us and instantly doze off. She would be performing salat and suddenly fall asleep. She would be eating and doze off.

Throughout her nearly thirty-plus years of battle with this disease, the latest development surprised everyone, including herself and her doctors. They would regularly check her vitals and say all appeared normal. They would run multiple scans and do bloodwork to analyze and deduce the source of her newly developed symptoms but to no avail. She always took her medication and observed a strict diet, but Momma's involuntary slumber only soared. Little did we know that this spontaneous sleep syndrome was death's emissary in slow action. It placed a transparent covering on our naked eyes and minds. Not a single soul could detect this sneaky symptom's root.

Her care team later assumed her glucose level was consistently low. We were asked to encourage her to increase her food consumption to help boost her blood sugar level. We did so and would sometime force her to eat a spoon of steamed couscous or chew on a plate of cucumber salad. Sadly, whatever went in rushed back out. Her stomach could no longer tolerate food. Her appetite had long been crushed by death's merciless envoy. Her journey to the spirit world was halfway complete.

PART FOUR

In Grief's Grip

This is certainly the coldest, emptiest, and darkest place on earth.

Death's ruthless winds ripped Momma from us when we least expected it. We weren't prepared. She was known for battling multiple health crises and coming back looking and feeling somewhat better. For us, it wasn't time. We needed her too much to lose her. It was a brutal reality to live with.

Momma was in great health before she turned thirty when her life began to spiral downward. She suffered from an incurable, deteriorating foot ulcer for decades. Doctors from near and far were unable to pinpoint the cause of her illness. They told us that her poor health was caused by a defect in insulin production in her pancreas. Pale and frail, she complained of blurred vision, excessive hunger, and frequent urination. She was always nauseous, shaky, sweating, and feeling chilly. In the weeks leading up to her death, I had a strange but recurring dream:

I was a tiny silver bird living in an orange ball where many other birds lived. We lived a happy life and had everything we wanted. One day, I noticed some ruffles on one side of our ball—the only home we had ever known. After studying it for a while, I called for backup. I was joined by my close friends:

Alimatou, Zahra, and Memounatou. We later discovered that there was a tiny crack in the ruffles through which air was escaping.

In the end, it deflated, resulting in the death of all my bird family except my best friends and me. We miraculously escaped through the pinched hole, only to be tossed into a larger, orange ball with millions of inhabitants who weren't birds. As time passed, I noticed my friends, and I were morphing into our new hosts—vertical creatures with two arms, two legs, a head (that comprised two eyes, a nose, a mouth, and two ears), and a tummy.

Unlike our previous ball, our new home was warmer, calmer, and greener. There was never a shortage of food or water for us. Mostly, we survived on nuts and fruits. Our needs were met in full. Then one day, a storm swept through our ball. This time, I was the only one affected. I was squeezed out of our beloved ball. I cried and tried my best to hold on to my friends. Unfortunately, I failed. There was a tremendous amount of pressure. A reddish tunnel lay ahead of me. I saw Alimatou, Zahra, and Memounatou crying in the distance. They screamed that they didn't want to be left alone, but we couldn't stop the tornado from pulling me through the tunnel.

The next morning, I felt undone. Despite being thankful that it was only a bad dream, I felt very uncomfortable in my own skin. My fear came from two sources: first, the idea that I had existed in two lives before and second, the question of why was I dreaming such a thing?

* * *

I was unaware of Momma's life-threatening health crisis on June 10, 2019. My siblings were horror-struck. Afraid I would hurt myself knowing Momma was lying still on a hospital bed, fighting for her life. Even so, I felt viciously uprooted and destroyed.

On that day, I woke up ruined, with a critical part of me missing. It felt strange and mysterious, but I attributed it to the nightmare I had experienced days earlier. Normally, I wouldn't have even given it a second thought since I was a deep sleeper.

As a child I was notorious for nightmares and feared thunder and lightning. My fear intensified on rainy nights when the seemingly massive southern skies were fully illuminated by a glimmer of raw light beaming through our blackout curtains. On such nights, I was awoken by the roaring boom that shook our home's ceilings.

I remember waking up to intense physical fights between myself and a force that I could never identify with my naked eye. I would walk out of bed the next morning covered in scratches on my neck, jaws, hands, and practically everywhere else. Momma would notice them and say, "Your *damasas* were here last night." I never asked what she meant.

On other nights, I awoke breathless because I had nightmares of innocent women and children being killed senselessly in the countryside. For wealth and fame, the dark-hearted masters of our land periodically offered these human sacrifices to mountain and valley dwarfs. Hundreds of defenseless residents of the hinterlands were murdered every day by ritual assassins. They mutilated their victims to death.

While still alive, victims' breasts, genitals, and tongues were extracted. Around the end of each year, between October and December, these vicious killings became more frequent. Children and vulnerable adults disappeared without a trace. Their mutilated bodies were later discovered on beaches, in bushlands, or by roadsides.

These happenings were a brute, underdiscussed truth about our society. Rural dwellers lived in complete fear for their entire lives. Good thing I had long moved to the cityside where these occurrences were nonexistent. Yet I endured occasional nightmares about these horrendous acts, followed by days of lightheadedness. However, the cruelty I endured on June 10 had zero roots in these dreams, though I insisted on holding them responsible.

I had lost my soul. Without it, I was meaningless, lost in a labyrinth of uncertainties. For the first time, I was *afraid of the unknown*.

*　*　*

I felt bruised inside, my mind wandered, and my heart exploded. *What's causing this sudden emptiness?* Aloud, I asked. *Could it be that my soul couldn't find its way back? In order for that to happen, I must be involved in sorcery.* True. Old witches were the only ones who had the power to do this. A soul *had* to leave its human form at ungodly hours in order to become owls, pythons, raccoons, and mermaids to cause mischief in the land. If a fellow witch desired revenge, they would flip the body upside down to confuse the soul and prevent it from returning. It was impossible for a soul to enter or return to a tempered home; the transition had to be smooth and unaffected.

As I pondered this, an ear-piercing hiss rose up inside me. My soul had no connection to the Dark World. Our society's bona fide witches were initiated by a family member or relative. It was a butchery club to which one needed to be invited by someone from within. It worked just like that. Hereditary. Dark magic would have been introduced to you by your uncle, mother, or father. There was only one other way to transfer sorcery outside of this famous genetic transfer: by unsolicited human flesh and blood— here's how that worked:

To lure you into the bloodsucking world of witchery, a witch would hand you meat chops to eat. Although they looked like mouthwatering lamb or beef chops to you, they were actually human flesh. As soon as you ate this, they came after your soul at night, demanding that you return the favor. They refused to accept real beef chops as repayment, claiming their meat was a special kind that could only be repaid by joining their ranks. They bugged you until you became a necromancer.

A mythical tale about a powerful teenage witch ran deep in our land. Maïmouna went to her neighbor's home to fetch charcoal beans.

Unsuspectingly, she knocked, was welcomed in, and shown to the fire in the backyard. Her path to the makeshift kitchen was interrupted when she saw meat chops on a barbeque grill outside the main door. She was offered a piece by her neighbor.

That night, Maïmouna's next-door neighbor and a crew of witches appeared in her dream, demanding a just recompense for the offer. Of course, no amount of beef or money could make up for what she had eaten. In this case, it was the flesh of her neighbor's firstborn son, offered as a lamb to fellow witches. Witchery was a payback club: if we ate mine, we had to eat yours. She eventually joined forces with established witches in her neighborhood. Together, they unleashed chaos on residents every night.

Thankfully, neither of these scenarios applied to me. So why would anyone or anything interfere with my soul? The answers I sought were everywhere except in the right places.

Having lost my heart, I was intolerant of the sucking dark hole that had replaced it. My anxiety was fueled by my tears. My chest bled, and my lungs were devoid of oxygen. As I gasped for air, it felt like something within me was dying.

*　*　*

I had experienced sorrow in all shapes and forms, but what I went through on June 10, 2019, was nothing compared to my previous encounters with grief. Momma's death wasn't my first loss, but it was the hardest. I was first exposed to grief when death yanked away my childhood friend. Bijou was a dark-skinned teenager with beautiful pop-eyes. A prominent definition of her modesty, humility, and dignity was her adamant love affair with the hijab. Despite her young age, she remained faithful to the veil for as long as she lived.

My friend died at a local hospital in Kissingburg on February 8, 2018, from pregnancy complications that could have been prevented had she received the right antenatal care throughout her pregnancy. She was in her seventh month, and due for a fourth child in April. Both lives were lost.

Bijou's pregnancy was marred by fluctuating blood pressure levels. Additionally, she suffered from severe nausea and vomiting. Like a thousand other expectant mothers in Kissingburg, Bijou barely accessed the recommended eight antenatal appointments throughout her pregnancy. This coastal village had one of the highest maternal mortality rates in the world. A woman or girl died every minute due to complications during pregnancy or childbirth. A staggering 2,072 maternal deaths per 100,000 births were recorded yearly in the area. Our mothers were terrorized by this scourge of death.

Granted, the conflict-ravaged society was still recovering from devastating tribal wars that had destroyed its health centers and road networks. However, the few renovated and operating health facilities were not within reach of the vast majority of the population. Only a handful of people lived less than one hundred kilometers from a health facility. This inaccessibility resulted in most births occurring at home, usually attended by unsupervised traditional midwives. This was common in remote areas where infrastructure and facilities were most lacking.

The disheartening truth is that most maternal deaths could have been prevented had the government ensured that expectant mothers' hopeless financial situations did not determine their pregnancies' outcomes. Bijou deserved better—not death while giving life. I suffered emotional torment after her death, but nothing compared to what I experienced on June 10. On this day, I suffered thirsty and unforgiving emotional pain.

PART FIVE

A Taste of Soullessness

Samira or Omar called me whenever Momma was battling a coma or had been rushed to a hospital, but June 10 was different. No one said a thing to me. Yet I was breathless. I felt every pain Momma felt without knowing what was unfolding back in Merrivylle.

I choked on my tears as I stared at the ceiling of my floral-adorned studio apartment overlooking the Ocean Lagoon. It didn't matter how beautiful this purple water was, the howling feeling that pinned me to the ground couldn't be calmed. It felt more like a loss of memory. I longed for the me who refused to accept grief, sadness, and sorrows as part of life. I wanted to get up and go, just like how our parents expected us to bounce right back after enduring grief. Despite my eagerness, grief forced me to recognize that living was a continuous learning experience.

*   *   *

Arms and legs flopping about like those of a useless scarecrow before reviving with goosebumps. I was possessed by a bloodthirsty nothingness. The harder I tried, the more soullessness I felt. I screamed softly because I lived in a *mind-your-own-business* apartment complex. I would not have received help even if I screamed, "HELP!" Such conduct was strictly prohibited and punishable by lengthy, rigid legal proceedings.

That's just how *Saboudou* functioned. Call it a strange society, but everyone here minded their own business. Neighborliness was inexistent. A century-old adage reinforced the notion that neighbors were never to be trusted. Folks avoided each other. They used smartphones, tablets, TVs, podcasts, and music to shift their attention from everyone else around them.

"You do not want to deal with those unneighborly behaviors. Just mind your own business, and you will be just fine," the leasing manager at Harris Inn informed me upon signing my five-year lease agreement.

Shooting him a quizzical look, I asked: "So if you were to trip and fall and cannot call 911 instantly, you just chill till death comes to your rescue?"

"Welcome to Cherry City," Darren said, flashing a sinister smile. "Everything here is different. Tribes, communities, and kin don't exist here. No one is a default extended family for anyone here. Individual privacy trumps all else. It is what matters the most to us. We must see that our tenants' privacy is protected, including yours, Ms. Lahai."

"This is best for all of us. Some neighbors can be downright snoopy, defiant, and even hostile." He paused for a quick breather. "With our *mind-your-own-business* policy in place, neighbor harassment is never a problem in our community."

I wasn't sure if that was meant to soothe the situation.

* * *

Even though locals here were aloof, they held a common belief that there was a Mighty Being to whom anyone could run for unlimited emotional and mental support. He was *The Perfect Therapist* to whom everyone was welcome to approach feeling outraged, irrational, childish, insecure, or irritable. He was *The Most Merciful*, with whom everyone could throw constant temper tantrums and never had to worry about hurting His feelings. He was the *Doctor of Souls* in whose healing powers everyone had uncontested faith and hope. If you needed emotional support, you privately went to Him. This Mighty Being was *The Most Caring*, the only Being that always demonstrated the willingness to help, was empathetic, and practiced mindful listening to the pains and sorrows of His subjects.

Nevertheless, locals only knew and needed Him when they were distressed. During their happy days, they had no sense of needing Him. Those who realized their faults and came racing to Him with remorse, gratitude, and praise were embraced with open arms. He was *The Most Beneficent*, the only Being who never slammed a door in your face in times of prosperity and troubles. So, residents knew where to go in search of mental stability. So simple, so straightforward.

Now you see why I didn't bother being loud on the morning of June 10. I knew no one would come to my aid save the red glow of the golden sun, with rays so notable and robust that they subdued the southern skies into bowing in complete submission. Not even my blackout curtains could resist the raging beams of this terrible, late morning sun.

I hated the raging inferno I woke up to. My shoulders could barely support my heavy head. It felt like a large bundle of wet firewood resting on my neck. The bleakness in my heart was crippling. Every breath weighed me down, sucking me further and further into the ground. This early grief was stiff, a mixture of passion and pain that was so tender to the touch. The agony was pure, honest, and relentless. And in it, I found deep comfort, drowning further and further into a pool of loathsome self-pity.

I fought a dismal war for my soul on June 10, hours before learning about Momma's passing. My hands were paralyzed due to panic attacks. My stomach chewed up its linings. "Somebody please help me! Anybody!"

* * *

I was halfway through the required paperwork for Momma to visit me in Cherry City. I needed her love, physically, around me. I wanted her to receive care there since medicine was very advanced in that part of the world. She loved the city's name. "Do you all have cherries blossoming in your homes?" she teased me. "I can't wait to experience the cherries of this great city."

Cherry City was indeed an architectural masterpiece. Its dazzling parks, historical monuments, enormous museums, superb buildings, and countless natural harbors caught your breath immediately. The city was the largest and busiest in *Saboudou*. There was one thing that made this city special: its office buildings, museums, airports, private homes, and train and bus stations were all designed in a revolutionary manner. The skyscrapers were environmentally friendly and turned heads. *Saboudou's* most diverse and populated city. The population density was more than fifteen thousand mixed people per square mile. In Cherry City, you could find almost every race and hear virtually any language. Some called it *home away from home*. The city was divided into five boroughs: Queens, La Rue du Jardin, Zone Quatre, Roxzy, and Boulevard Verte. I loved it there because it was refreshingly beautiful.

PART SIX

Take a Bow

Skin layered with ice, fingers numb and tingling like the carpal tunnel syndrome experienced during pregnancy. In my mind's eye, I saw Momma fully veiled in a stainless robe. She was lying with her face turned directly into the red sunset. I ran to her. She turned but frowned. The closer I got to her, the more her frown expanded, as though she was trying to tell me something with her eyes. When I got closer, she shook her head, got up, and walked away.

That was the last straw! Hands shaking, I dialed my sister's number. The call failed. My credits were out. My bank account was in the red. I sat motionless. Then my phone started blinking. It was Binta, my friend.

"I need to make a quick call home."

"Is everything okay? How's Momma doing?"

"I don't know. I've been feeling very sick all day. I need to check on her, but my Boss Revolution account is in the red."

"Of course, it has to be. You spend too much money on international calls. Keep making that company rich with your daily spending of $80 on calls." I was guilty of overspending on phone cards, but I couldn't resist doing so. I had to hear from Momma every second of my day. Unfortunately, the phone she had wasn't WhatsApp compatible at the time. We only chatted through WhatsApp when Samira was around.

"Binta, you don't have to remind me. Just send me the twenty-dollar credits. I will reimburse you on Friday."

"I will, but don't you think twenty dollars is too much for a one-time top-up?"

"And which part of that concerns you? The money? Or the frequency? Do you even understand the urgency of this call?" Binta was too stubborn. I loved her profoundly but was intolerant of her judgmental approach to matters.

"Did you get the message?"

"Wait, let me check. Okay, yes, I see it. Thanks. I will pay you on Friday."

"You don't have to. Just take care of yourself. Call me if you need me. Oh…let me know what you find out."

I dropped my phone and took several deep breaths before dialing Samira's number again. Still her line was not going through. "She hasn't paid her phone bill again," I thought. I dialed Momma's number. It rang, but there was no answer. I felt a dull punch in my chest. My stomach heated up. My abdomen contracted as though I was six centimeters dilated in active labor without the help of an epidural.

I dialed Omar's number. He picked up. I asked for Momma; he froze. I sensed it. My tough-talking big brother was afraid of speaking to me.

"Where's Momma? How's she doing?" I asked warily.

"Ugh. Ugh," went Omar, stammering.

"I'm listening," I said, letting him know that my blood had drained out and that I was now surviving on the last drop.

"Why are you stammering? Are you trying to hide something from me?"

"Ugh. Manatou. Ugh."

"You are making me scared. Your hesitance is making me anxious."

"Okay…you know…the thing is…."

"What thing is? Could you please tell me if everything is okay with Momma?"

"Well, remember, she's also my mom."

"Then, what the HECK is going on with her?!" I screamed.

"We are back at the hospital."

He finally spilled it, sending trillions of shockwaves down my spine. My comfy office chair was suddenly sultry. My hair strands crawled from end to end, extended in length and wrapped themselves into bundles of petite reptiles like those of Medusa.

"What did you say?! Can I speak to her? What are the doctors saying?" I was a rigid bully when it came down to Momma's health. I was persistent, pushy, and controlling. I was never ashamed of it, nor did I bother to hide it. I was willing and happy to sacrifice all I had ever gained, including my life, to nurse Momma back to life. I had zero regrets for doing what I had to do to help Momma.

I insisted on getting tangible results, regardless of what that meant. I was crazy about Momma. She was all I had, a valuable piece of my heart and soul. Momma was the keeper of my smiles and the knower of my pain. She was the receiver of my sorrow and the igniter of my joy.

*   *   *

No medical bill was too heavy to carry as long as it meant Momma would be okay and able to speak and crack jokes with me again. I prayed for longevity for Momma and did all sorts of odd jobs to legitimately raise funds to pay her medical costs, ensuring that she accessed the best care—and on time. I *had* to because, in Merrivylle, only a handful of elites had the right to and could afford health insurance. The bulk of the population, including my family, was miserably poor and compelled to pay out-of-pocket and upfront before accessing care, regardless of a patient's medical condition. It didn't matter if your patient was dying; you *had* to pay the full cost of care before the patient's vitals were even taken. Even if your patient was transported to a hospital by an ambulance, you were still compelled to join an endless queue of outpatients to see a doctor. No one cared about the life-threatening condition of your patient in urgent need of care, hence the reason for an ambulance in the first place.

Besides, ambulatory services didn't signify urgency or emergency in most parts of Merrivylle. No matter how loud an ambulance screamed down the road, motorists did not care, though there existed laws that any emergency vehicle with its lights and sirens on had the right of way. The laws were, however, never enforced; they were stacked up on shelves, collecting dust.

That's where your troubles as a patient's family began. And if you were unlucky enough to meet the doctors and nurses on the other side of the professional curve, you, your patient or your loved ones were doomed. Your desperateness was exploited: bills blown out of proportion, increased unprofessionalism, and hostility replaced your right to on-time and effective service to save lives. It could start with "We have no beds available" and end with "Take your patient home. We cannot see him/her today." Nurses screamed at and belittled patients at will; doctors were bent on devious deals, such as forcing patients into seeking service or care at their privately run clinics. We were forced to triple the cost of care at private clinics because the so-called medical doctors would not see Momma at major referral hospitals where the government subsidized services.

Doctors employed by the government at public referral hospitals stole critical equipment from those hospitals to establish their private clinics and used the public hospitals to source clients. If you took your patient to the hospital, they diverted you to their private clinics, where they charged you significantly.

Honestly, I didn't care about their dirty deeds. I remained steadfast and would move mountains to see Momma's health restored. I loved her to pieces, which strengthened me to ignore the fact that doctors and health workers were exploiting me.

* * *

"What are the doctors saying?!"

"She…she…ate. And…she's now resting."

"I asked what are the doctors saying?"

"Ugh…we got her a private room, and doctors are warning us against disrupting her sleep," said Omar, struggling to compose himself.

"WHAT ARE THE DOCTORS SAYING?!"

"Calm down, Manatou. Momma is sleeping."

"So why is no one picking up my calls? If all is well with her, if she's only sleeping in a hospital's private room instead of her bedroom, then why is no one talking to me? What would anyone feeling okay be doing in a hospital sleeping? Omar, stop the joke. Where is she?!" I screamed, hopping from end to end. Then suddenly and very strangely, Omar went downhill.

"Ugh, she just finished eating."

"Wait a minute," I said interrupting, but Omar ignored me and went on.

"Ugh, I'm at the mini mart getting her some eggs to eat."

He sounded positively devious, trying so hard to conceal either his pain or a piece of severely devastating news from me. My siblings were notorious for keeping secrets from me whenever breaking news happened in the family, and I happened to be at work.

I got nothing from Omar. That night, I sat with the phone in my hands, waiting to make another call. I was desperate to speak with my sweet Momma.

* * *

Allãnoor Abdoule Lahai, my beautiful Momma, was born on June 8, 1959 in the sparkly village of Harper, Fasso Province. She was born to peasant farmers and petty traders. Her father, Mèmè, was a renowned subsistent farmer, and her mother, Rokia, was well-known for her snack smart business. Sankaraka, a gas-filled mountain, stood tall in their town. My grandparents farmed the land directly beneath this mountain. It was an area seldom harvested by most of humanity. Dark spirits possessed the area, but a daring spirit equally guided Mèmè. Throughout his life, he denied fear a chance to bar him from reaching his goals. His family's survival depended hugely on farming, and he wouldn't allow fear to paralyze him.

The area was cold, dark, echoey, and creepy. Farmlands were specks of gold dust in this town; they were scarce and expensive. In some areas, they required human sacrifices. The land beneath Sankaraka was free, provided you didn't interfere with a silver stool that sat atop this hair-raising mountain. Mèmè knew this from his forebears. It was a buried family secret transferred from one generation to the other. He avoided being tempted by this alluringly magical artwork.

He was a fearless hunter and spent a hefty portion of his time cultivating golden rice fields, vegetables, and fruits. He was also obsessed with sugar cane; and therefore, invested some time into growing this grass for home consumption only. *Moin* Rokia and her cowives, Aïsha and Fadëema, spent time cultivating peanut fields, roots, and tubers.

Momma was the second baby girl born to the Abdoules. The first was Tantie Maï, a slender girl with naturally silver hair right from birth. Momma's hair was golden. Her age-defying, coffee-colored skin was mind-blowing. Her almond-shaped eyes were brownish and attention-grabbing. She was chubby and medium built.

* * *

Momma had twenty-one siblings—twelve brothers and nine sisters. She demonstrated exceeding talent for entrepreneurialism early in life. She sold produce from her family's farm to raise extra money for their upkeep. At age six, her father enrolled her in school with her male siblings. It was a bold decision at the time. Girls were forbidden from seeking education; it was the right of boys only, but Mèmè saw it differently. With proceeds from farm harvest, he paid for their education. At age fifteen, Momma was married to a man she barely knew but later grew fond of. She remained thankful to her parents for connecting her with her ultimate soulmate.

Harôon Lahai was a thriving businessman and my dearest Papa. Their union was blessed with three girls—Samira, Manatou, and Tantie—and three boys—Omar, Khalil, and Ahmed. Tantie and Ahmed died as infants. Our home thrived on respect, honesty, and accountability. Momma was a devoted wife. She upheld her marriage vows until her last breath. Papa predeceased her. She was only thirty-two years old then, but Momma never remarried. Not because she never had suitors. Highly influential men competed for her hand in marriage.

Her commitment to staying engaged with Papa's family was even more intriguing. She ensured that we knew who we were, where we originated from, who Papa's siblings were, and what they did for a living. If it weren't for her persistence, we would have all grown up not knowing a thing about our paternal family.

"Take this number and make sure to call and say hello."

"Whose number is this again?" I would ask.

"It belongs to your father's only sister. Remember to check in with her once in a while."

My ancestors weren't from the same area. My mom's parents were northerners, and my dad's parents were westerners. Momma helped us navigate our way inside the family by tracing our roots, helping us to understand, appreciate, and cherish wholeheartedly our ancestral history.

Momma didn't limit her love for children to just us. She cherished the children of other people, sometimes total strangers. She made them feel like they were hers and was the best friend of nearly every youth in the community. Occasionally we, her belly-born, were jealous that she was putting other kids before us. "Every good I am doing for other people's children shall be repaid to you all in due course, most likely when I'm no longer around. You may not see it coming. It will happen at times when you least expect it," she told us.

She never meddled in our personal lives but always gave advice and was there for us when we needed her. We shared a strong tie and kept nothing from each other. I felt very comfortable having difficult conversations with her about challenges in my life. Keeping secrets from her fueled my insecurity. She maintained the first place on my speed dial. Siri was very familiar with all things Momma. We were connected in heart and mind. Momma loved soccer. I developed similar affection for the game so we could share the fun. We looked forward to the Cup of Nations and the World Cup games. I would intentionally go against the team she was rooting for to spice up our soccer moments further. Our bond was beautifully irrational.

* * *

Unlike her peers, Momma was never afraid of confessing her deep love for us. She told us, "I love you" daily. Back then most parents never told their children they loved them. It was considered taboo. And while her peers grappled with the spending guilt, Momma was never guilty about spending lavishly on our wardrobes. Samira wore some of the costliest wax fabrics as a teen. Momma also furnished her girls with raw gold earrings that we wore on special occasions, such as Eid.

Some of my friends complained that their mothers neglected them inadvertently while caring for their siblings. They said it was impossible for a mother to love all her children equally. That no matter how hard she masked her deep love for one child, there were ways that it popped up. That most moms weren't accountable for such divisive actions. Well, my Momma proved this wrong. She loved her children evenly, reducing the tendency of sibling rivalry among us. You would think I was the most loved if you met her with me. If you saw her with Samira, you would think she was Momma's favorite child. Don't get me started on her deep affection for Omar and Khalil. She loved everything her children ever loved, even if she disapproved. The gentlest soul ever to walk the earth.

* * *

Her almond-shaped eyes added a touch of fierceness to her striking look. Her inherited confidence (from her Momma) and self-love were beyond measure. Momma loved to smile, enjoyed laughing, and always sought ways to share her positive vibes. "Smiles are a charity," she often said. True. Momma was a charitable organization in human form. There were times when she had to walk through hell to serve humanity. During the 1998 tribal war in Merrivylle, Momma put her life on the line, walked on beds of death traps, and dodged bullets and arrows across rebel lines to search for food and to bring her family and friends to safety. Even those dwelling in various refugee camps were brought to stay in our compound. She put everyone's needs before hers and was so sympathetic that she often forgot that the word "no" even existed.

Momma struggled to make time for herself and always tended to her children, siblings, and friends before herself. No doubt, whenever I thought of her, I thought of these words: self-sacrificing and robust. She was never interested in serving others to be recognized. Giving was part of her life; it was stuffed in her D.N.A. Omar's friends, the majority of whom belonged to well-off families, came running to Momma for clothes, cash, and time donations. Not that their parents couldn't afford to provide for them.

Momma taught us the gift of giving and the need to treat others with dignity, respect, kindness, and love. She proved it was possible to be mighty and scared at the same time, cautioning us against surrendering to road-blocks (visible and invisible) on our paths to success.

"Never bow to walls you must climb to reach your goal," she said. She taught us never to be afraid of shedding tears when we had to but to ensure that we never stopped until we made it.

PART SEVEN
Unbearably Bitter

"Manatou, I need your address," his voice came through, emotionless. I said nothing. My cousin Bilal was usually nice, but we rarely talked or interacted. Receiving a call from him at 11:59 p.m. on June 10 was telling.

"I'm booked for a ride to Blitzville. I will be spending the night with you all," Bilal continued, ignoring the silence on my end. My eyes popped out of their sockets. I stood—said nothing. Then he went, "Hello? Hello? Hello? Ugh. I guess I lost her." The call went dead.

Bilal's call triggered instant diarrhea. On my fourth trip to the restroom, I sat on the commode for several minutes, thinking: "We hardly talk. Bilal never calls me, and when he does, it's during the weekend. Why today? Why now? Why is he even dropping a client in Blitzville this late? Is this some sort of a prank? Why would he even think of pranking me tonight?" I grumbled; my heart leapt to my mouth.

A few minutes later, I saw a text coming through: "Our line got disconnected. Please text me your address. I'm on my way to you." Reluctantly I obliged. Not because I didn't want him over. The timing of his visit was wrong. Blitzville was only fifteen minutes away from Cherry City but an hour away from Pittsburgh, Bilal's city of residence.

* * *

Bilal arrived at my Flower Valley home at 2:50 a.m. He headed upstairs into the guestroom but never slept. At 6:00 a.m., he was at my door, knocking softly.

"Manatou. Manatou."

"I knew it! Bilal's visit here is bad news personified. What does he want now?" I said softly.

"Manatou? Wake up. I'm returning to Pittsburgh this morning."

With shockwaves racing up my spine, I asked, "Really? Why so early?"

"I have an urgent meeting to attend," he responded, struggling to conceal a sharp dreariness in his voice. I could hear it. I could feel it. And I H-A-T-E-D it.

"Did you hear me?"

"Yes. Just a second. Let me make breakfast for you."

"No. You don't have to," Bilal declined almost immediately and yet politely. "Don't worry about it. I will grab something along the way. Besides I'm not a breakfast person."

"Well, you can't just leave on an empty stomach. Have you forgotten what our old folks say about skipping breakfast?"

"Of course not. I just don't feel like eating yet."

"'Breakfast drives away Satan,' they say. So allow me to make you a cup of coffee or tea with some lime."

"Okay. No problem. But what's taking you so long? I need you outside now. Please come out. COME OUTSIDE! Please," he insisted, his voice trembling.

I was still snuggled under my batik-printed blanket, wide awake but paralyzed by the uncertainties that marred my previous day, his odd appearance, and now his mood. I dragged myself out of bed, threw on a shawl, and headed out. As I stepped through my bedroom door, Bilal seized my left arm and led me into the guestroom.

"Sit," he ordered, pointing at the puffy, ruffle-free queen bed.

"What's wrong?" I asked, looking directly into his eyes.

"What's wrong?" I repeated, taking a few steps backward.

"What happened? Where's Allãnoor?"

I made a U-turn and headed downstairs. There an even bigger surprise awaited me. Myriame and her son-in-law were seated on the sofa, wearing terror looks. Seeing them amplified my worries. My gut feeling told me something had happened to Momma. I made another turn and headed for the main door. *Where was I going?* I don't know. Probably into the streets like the mentally unstable woman I had been for the past twenty-four hours. Bilal crossed ahead and redirected me into the living room. He looked at me and broke down in tears.

"What is it?" I asked, bursting into tears. At this point, I needed it. I needed to cry loud and long. I was tired of suppressing it.

"It's Allãnoor…" he began but paused immediately. I pushed his hands off my shoulder, walked away from him looking villainous. Bilal tried getting closer to me. He knew the look in my eyes was painfully sad, suicidal even. I retreated as he advanced towards me, leaving a reasonable distance between us. I had no idea what I was about to unleash. Internally I knew what I wanted: B-L-O-O-D!

* * *

"Manatou, Allãnoor is gone. Her Creator called on her, and she peacefully responded," Bilal said. I froze. Suddenly I felt my heart ripped before I passed out.

"I knew it! This girl is going to die!" Bilal screamed.

"You can't break down too, Bilal," Duke intoned. "We all need to be very strong for her."

"Fetch me some water," Myriame ordered.

"For what?" asked Bilal, looking surprised.

"To sprinkle fresh water on her. You don't expect us to sit here and watch her in this dormant state without helping."

"How about CPR?" Bilal proposed.

"Then why haven't you done that? I will sprinkle some fresh water on her to help her regain consciousness. That's how we, the traditional people, do it," Myriame said.

"I'm calling 911," Duke interrupted.

"To do what?" Myriame asked, visibly upset.

"To save a dying soul."

"On whose account?" she asked.

"What do you mean?"

"I mean, who is paying for that ambulance…that costly ride?" Myriame was relentless.

"Do you have any idea of her financial burden and how adding unnecessary bills from an ambulance ride would further cripple her ability to take care of her mom's funeral rites?"

"Oh, we should let her die because we are afraid of an ambulance bill? Which is which? Her life or the money?" Duke shot back.

"You are such a clueless human being."

"That's fine, but you are outraged due to a personal experience of yours that's possibly an isolated case," Duke added, setting Myriame's temper on fire.

"Oh? Since when did being slammed with an unexpected bill of $5,650 for a six-mile ambulance ride become normal? Yes, I'm furious because I believe these services should be FREE. Some of our tax monies should be used for these emergency services."

As they argued, Bilal entered the kitchen and filled a plastic bowl with cold water from the sink. He got a face towel from my room, soaked it, and began massaging my face. I was semi responsive by then. A tingling yet numbing and burning sensation altered my face. My facial capillaries were dilating fast. For hours, my face remained red and tingly. My eyes hurt excruciatingly. My lips bled from me chewing on them.

* * *

Momma had embarked on a very long voyage. Some called it the ultimate journey of no return. It meant there would be no more midday calls from her, no birthday songs for me from her, no more being merry in my world. All these feelings went along with her, in addition to my hopes, dreams, heart, and soul.

Bilal had traveled overnight from Pittsburgh to Cherry City to bring me distant news that no one in the universe could convey over the phone. No one had the courage to do so, not even my siblings. Everyone understood the mother-daughter bond between Momma and me. Yet they were also worried that I would stumble upon this news on social media if they delayed telling me. At the time, social media platforms, especially Facebook, were notorious for unwarranted obituaries. You would bump into images of loved ones decorated with *RIP* hashtags anytime.

Nothing hurt like finding out about the death of a loved one on social media through strangers turned death-announcers. They announced some deaths in less than five minutes of the incident. No one cared about a grieving family's privacy. No one considered *what* or *when* it was appropriate to post certain things, especially death news. Grieving families were left at the mercy of such unscrupulous folks—all in the name of wanting to be up-to-date with a rapidly evolving digital age.

I learned of the passing of Tantie Rougie through Facebook, and I nearly cracked my skull in shock. It took me three weeks to process and learn to live with this emotional terror. Had it been the traditional way, I would have been mentally prepared to receive it, deal with it, and peacefully depart from it. Traditionally, before death news was announced, you were mentally prepared. You were reminded of *your* purpose in this life and the fact that every soul was bound to taste death at an appointed time. This is how it was done in Merrivylle.

* * *

Bilal tried reinforcing his words of comfort. I was still emotionally unresponsive. I remained on the floor for twenty minutes before regaining full consciousness. I rolled myself up and stared deeply into everyone's eyes as if to say, *did you all hear what was said?* Gradually, I transitioned to a sitting position but still couldn't cry. My skin and face burned. The heat from within and outside my body numbed my heart to everything happening around me.

I sat briefly before soliloquizing: "That was never a part of our plan. She can't betray me. She knows I am coming. She's waiting to see me. I miss her. She misses me. Oh, wait, what did I do wrong? Where did I go wrong? What could I have done differently? I hate me!"

I ran down the street like a headless chicken, falling, getting back up, and falling again—my knees, arms, and fingers all bruising from being smashed against the asphalt. I was still in my nightgown, my hair wrapped in a sleeping bonnet, and I had no slippers on. Someone was calling my name, but I couldn't tell who or what it was. I kept running toward the call, causing drivers to slam on their brakes. Bilal and Duke chased me, but I was faster than a flash of lightning during a thunderstorm.

I soon found a faceless figure standing in the heart of my neighborhood street. It was darker than night yet very shimmery. It opened its arms for a warm hug, and I disappeared into its bosom. I walked through a door and heard the voices of humans and animals. Tweets of birds roared through the winds. Joyful cries of babies captured the skies. Cozy winds combed through pinkish pine trees. Nothing here looked familiar: the grass was greener, thicker, and thorny. The air was as sweet as sugar. It was a painless, griefless place with valleys filled with sparkly rivers. I loved it and wished to dwell there for eternity.

Then I felt fingers threading through my hair, leaving an unbearable pinching sensation. I opened my eyes only to see myself reclining in my bedroom. "She has opened her eyes!" I heard Bilal screaming on the phone. "Here speak to her," he said, handing me his phone. Samira was on the line.

"Manatou? Manatou? Are you there?" I said nothing. "Momma says, 'Hello.' Manatou, Momma says, 'Thank you.'"

I smashed the phone into the wall and ran to my neighborhood's Giant store. In my head, Momma's medical bills were due. The sooner I was at the Western Union counter to send the funds to Merrivylle, the better. I sped off on foot, dodging between cars.

"It's an emergency. Allānoor's medicines are her life-support. You have to let me go. I have to be at the Western Union counter before they close. I can't be late. Let me goooooo!" I cried. Bilal and Duke looked at each other and shook their heads as if to say, *are you crazy?* And, yes, that was my current mental state. Then they said, "Manatou, you have to accept that Allānoor is no more. The sooner you accept it, the better." Of course. I wish I could, but how? Was it that easy?

* * *

Back then our people made no space or time for grief. Heeding anguish was a sign of weakness for some, even if that meant you would bleed internally for eternity. It started with openly discussing difficult emotions. We were chastised for doing so. Growing up in such a chaotic society, kids like me learned how to swallow our feelings and numb our hearts early on.

Nevertheless, grief couldn't be repressed. We would later come face-to-face with the painful reality of our repressed emotions as young adults. By then our thought patterns and behaviors would have been controlled and defined by stifled emotions. Sadly our folks didn't care about such a long-term impact of suppressed grief on one's mental health and physical well-being.

* * *

The cold winds of death blew off the lone light of my life. "No! No! Allānoor is not gone!" I screamed and passed out again. A dense mass stuck in my lungs had me fighting for my breath. I regained consciousness and wanted to run out again. Three hours later, I broke down. I cried hard, very loudly, nonstop for four hours—from 11:00 a.m. through 3:00 p.m.—peaking at 3:00 p.m. before transitioning into soft but profuse sobs. My guests stayed for two more days before returning to their homes in Pittsburgh and the Big Apple. It was then that grief became ruthless with me. I was lost at sea and had no idea when I would be rolled up in angry waves or for how long I would be held captive.

Momma's death stripped me of my identity, my autonomy. With her went my safety and security. I was vulnerable, and life did a fantastic job of exploiting my unprotected state. Her death altered my perspective on life for good. I had spent more than a quarter-century trying to live life on my own terms. Her passing instilled fear in me, the fear of life itself. Life was now unsafe and unworthy of my trust, poisoning my mind and relationship with everyone who cared about me. Inside me now dwelled a fire-breathing dragon, fueling self-hatred and hatred for others. My body was the home of self-aggression and misery.

* * *

Grief, regardless of its triggers, was impatient. It hit like a fussy newborn or a controlling newlywed desperately needing complete attention. You had to grieve *first*, then *move* on. There was no better way around this formula. So I made space for it. Because I adored Momma fiercely, grief, in my case, was generally inconsiderate. It stubbornly demanded to be honored. It destroyed my humanity.

I blocked my home and cell phone numbers to avoid getting calls from friends and relatives. I deactivated my social media and professional networking accounts, disabled my emails, and went into total lockdown, confined to my apartment. I would be smiling one second and foggy the next minute. I craved two things: sleeping and dreaming. I wanted to sleep for as long as possible, never wanting to wake up. I also longed to see and speak to Momma in my dreams, ask for her forgiveness, and pray for peace in her new home. I yearned to see her and prayed for her to no longer taste or feel pain and suffering. In my isolation, I drew closer to my Maker, praying religiously and asking Him to please forgive Momma's earthly shortcomings, widen and shed perpetual light in her grave, and grant her the highest level of *Al Jannat*.

I was grumpy when she didn't appear in my dreams within the first seven days of her passing. I didn't get a chance to see her before her demise. And now that she was gone, all I craved was the opportunity to say, "I love you; please forgive my shortcomings in the discharge of my duties to you as your child, and may Allah bless you with eternal peace." I grew angrier at myself and hated my new status—an orphan. My heart ached whenever people said, *may Allah forgive her* in reference to Momma. Not because I didn't want those prayers for her gentle soul but because I didn't want to accept her death. For days, I failed to mention Momma's name. Because now, saying her name meant adding this exact phrase: *May Allah forgive her*. Momma's name would never be cited or mentioned without this accompanying phrase, reminding me of her absence. In my life, there were no more extended highs, just low, lower, and lower. I said this prayer each night before returning to my solitary confinement:

O'Allah, please forgive Momma and grant her Al Jannat (Heaven). She was a devoted mother, sister, friend, and wife and would be fondly remembered by all who met and interacted with her. I miss her dearly, but I know she lived a life full of love for family and friends, laughter, generosity, and unwavering faith. May You be pleased with her gentle soul and grant her peace in her final resting place. Aameena.

I was trapped in my bedroom, bathroom, and clouded mental space. Life was useless. I missed Momma so much, yet I was denied a chance to see her again. This self-pity empowered grief to destroy me beyond compare. Though she was in Merrivylle, Momma had always been with me in Cherry City. She went to work with me daily, conversing with me throughout my journey to work. It was a voluntary, full-time job that she took on with exceeding passion. She called me at noon every day of my workweek to check on me. She had always waited until 1:00 p.m. to call me on my day off and stayed connected with me throughout the afternoon. These were only a few reasons why losing my Momma exposed me to a grief marathon: weeping for hours, battling lost appetite, and recurring sleeplessness while nursing multiple panic attacks.

The thought of her smiles had my stomach clenching. I listened to her last voicemail left on my phone, "Manatou. I am doing much better today. Don't worry too much. I will be fine. Let's be thankful and prayerful." I felt seas of chills racing down my spine. Some days, my mind and heart waged racing marathons. I would hear an amplified heartbeat in my ears and feel my body so electrified.

* * *

51

I indulged my fellow motherless sympathizers rather than those I considered "blessed" because they had zero idea of what I was going through. I would engage this group of sympathizers with direct eye contact, though my ears were locked to whatever they had to say.

When I transitioned to wailing, my family was hard on me, and it felt like being between a rock and a hard surface. "It is religiously offensive" to lament the death of a loved one, relatives told me. "When grieving takes the form of complaining, or when it becomes a prolonged expression of dissatisfaction, *that's* a problem," they said. Islam didn't forbid grieving the death of a beloved. It allowed us to do so by weeping, but not to the point of wailing and lamenting like I was doing.

"Wailing," they complained, "is an indirect manifestation of denial." They had a point there though. I was in complete denial for more than two years before transitioning to debating the next steps.

"Wailing means you are questioning Allah's will. Who are you to question His will? How dare you?!" they would say angrily. This worked wonders by reactivating my sense of religious reasoning, but it wasn't effective.

"The endless crying will only hurt your Momma. Don't you wish for her to have eternal peace in her grave? Your tears are toxic to her. She is awakened in her tomb and tormented each time you open your mouth to cry." These statements struck a chord, considering my immense love for Momma. I never wished for her to suffer, not in this worldly life or the hereafter. I hated to hear of her pain, let alone to be the orchestrator of her suffering. I wish I knew how to function on my own. I craved a brain that could fuel me with consistent positive energy to help me celebrate Momma's life instead of continuously wailing. Grieving, at this point, was an involuntary reaction on my part.

PART EIGHT
Peace, Not Pain

My family could no longer condone my tears. Some even kept a distance from me. Others called and added to my pain with their anger. I didn't blame anyone for reacting the way they did. I just wished they were more empathetic and understanding. "The souls of departed loved ones are tormented by the wailing of relatives. What is it about this that you don't get?" asked Omar as we spoke over the phone. "You can replace the wailing by dwelling on the good deeds of Momma. She was a woman with a perfect heart. She loved her family, her children, the children of other people, her siblings, and her community. So, please do not subject her to pain. She deserves *peace, not pain*."

"All she needs from you are prayers for her Creator to forgive her shortcomings and grant her paradise," urged Samira, joining in from the other line. "Instead of crying and being perpetually sad, you should use that energy to do more charitable deeds and ask Allah to transmit those blessings to Momma in her grave."

Okay. I got it, but was this enough to make bidding farewell to Momma any easier? I say NO! It only made me resentful, and I let my pain define my life out of resentment. I ignored my family's soaring frustration. I must admit that I did try to heed their pressure by hiding my grief along the way, but that only angered me to no limits, and out of anger came chaotic crabbiness.

Some days, I would bounce up from bed and peep through the thick curtains lining my large glass windows to see what message the late morning sun had brought from the heavens for me. On other days, I would fall back prostrate, letting down my guard and allowing my tears to reign. I cried on the carpet, on the bed, over the commode, in the closet, and in the shower. Even when I finally stepped out of my self-imposed lockdown, I still cried, sometimes with my sister, Samira. My throat was bruised, and my heart and head ached. Yet I didn't stop crying.

Grief lingered longer. Momma's death was a massive deconstruction of my life, and nothing ever mattered. I was *S-O-U-L-L-E-S-S.*

* * *

Three weeks later, I bounced up one Monday afternoon and headed to work. I found my desk overwhelmed by assorted golden flowers blossoming cheerfully. A few mountains of costly Hallmark cards also lined the front of my keyboard. My coworkers had gone above and beyond to purchase and ink the cards with deep thoughts to uplift my spirit and encourage me to give life a second chance.

Yakub wrote: "It sucks to lose a parent, let alone a mother, the custodian of our souls. I lost my mom fifteen years ago. Yet it feels like seconds ago. You are in my thoughts."

LaTasha wrote: "My deepest condolences to you and your family. Please know that we are your family and are here to support you in any way we can."

Hamza wrote: "I am here for you. You are not alone. My heart is weighty, and I know yours is too."

Hafsa wrote: "My dearest Manatou, I am so sorry for your loss. Lots of love and healing vibes!"

Maymunah wrote: "I'm holding you in my heart, never letting you go through this all by yourself. I'm in this with you."

Rayhana wrote: "My heart hurts so much to hear of your loss. I'm praying for you day and night."

Safiyya wrote: "I know how you loved and celebrated your Momma. I was saddened, so saddened to hear of her passing—what a piece of shocking news! Manatou, my heart goes out to you at this time of grief."

These gestures worked magic, though very briefly. I knew my recovery would never be a quick fix. Grief, in my case, was so rigid. My pain was directly proportional to my love for Momma. It was the kind of pain that never, ever went away. With time, the howling soreness lessened to random roars. It worsened each night upon returning home from work.

* * *

"Stop the tears. Momma doesn't need those," Samira would say, coming after me for my watery eyes. "All Momma needs now is prayer. Besides… remember that she's always with us."

"If she *is* with me, then why am I *still* feeling miserably lonely? Why can't I talk to her? Why can't I even see her in my dreams?! It's nearly two months since she departed this world!"

"She will only let you see her if you are kind to her," according to Samira, who believed my continuous crying was driving Momma away. "Tears are a punishment that no deceased person deserves."

"How or what can I do to encourage her to appear to me?"

"Be good. Do good. Preach good. Stop harming her with your tears," noted Samira. "As I've always told you, doing a lot of good deeds and asking Allah to transmit those blessings to her is the best thing you can do for her." Samira also added that I could demonstrate kindness to Momma by "praying religiously and asking Allah to expand, lighten up her grave, and grant her eternal peace."

"Your tears won't bring her back. She was kind to you. Don't repay her kindness with sheer wickedness," Samira stressed. She had a point there. Yet the bottomlessness of my pain was a clear testament to the love I shared with Momma. I didn't ever expect to get to a point in life where I would be all right with the fact that my cheerful Momma was no more.

PART NINE

Road to Recovery

I had been approved for up to twelve weeks of job-protected leave long before Momma's death. My leave was scheduled to begin on May 30. My flight was booked. Luggage stacked up. Goodie bags for relatives were stuffed to their brims. Momma was with me virtually every step of the way, including visits to Best Buy, Macy's, Marshalls, DSW, Apple stores, ZARA, H&M, Costco, Bath and Body Works, and Bed, Bath & Beyond.

Two large suitcases were loaded precisely for Momma with 100 percent comfy loungewear, comfy shoes, authentic hijabs, and accessories, premium quality abayas, and a diamond necklace from Zales with her name etched upon it, among other fun stuff. The suitcases were each thirty-two inches long, nineteen inches wide, and twelve inches deep. Three additional large bags were stuffed with assorted giveaways: 100 percent cotton towel sets, dozens of dental care items, body lotion, deodorant, makeup sets, hair care products, bedding, footwear, handbags, MacBook Pros, iPhones, iPads, Samsung tablets, android devices, Bose speakers, among many others.

Everything went as planned until May 25, when I realized my leave start date had been miscalculated. Eight paid weeks left me with an additional four weeks of unpaid leave. I had saved up enough to cover only two of those four weeks. I couldn't afford to roll back on my time off. I needed twelve weeks.

There were no direct flights between *Saboudou* and Merrivylle. A roundtrip was seven days of being in the air or languishing at various international airports. I still needed to work an additional two weeks to ensure there was no break in Momma's care while I was away from work, and the checks had stopped showing up in my account.

I had a lengthy talk with my supervisor about extending my Family Medical Leave Act (FMLA) start date to June 6. She was very understanding and later informed me that she was inspired by my willingness to sacrifice everything to cater to Momma. "Not many people do this nowadays. I have come across well educated, wealthy people who care very little about family. I have worked with selfish, self-centered souls, which has altered my view of the world and human relationships. But you have proven otherwise. Here you are, pushing your leave back to raise additional funds, not for a holiday getaway or summer cruise through Venice or the Atlantis, but to care for the medical needs of your mother. Indeed, you are an inspiration," she explained.

* * *

From one issue to the other, the trip was moved to July 4. Momma and I finalized the booking process together. I sent her a copy of my itinerary, and she was ready to be at the airport to receive me. While I busied myself with preparing what I thought I wanted, how I wanted it to unfold, and when, Allah, *The Perfect Planner*, was busy designing a better plan. He didn't plan for my reunion with Momma. No wonder my trip kept bumping into glitches—one after the other. Why would He prevent such a meeting? I still don't know, and I dare not question His will.

I hadn't seen Momma in seven years. We longed for each other. A major event had happened in my life without her. All the wanting and desiring made this trip very special, but Allah's all-knowing. Probably He knew my grief would have been a million times more excruciating had I been present on the ground during Momma's transition to the otherworld. He knew that I would have never forgiven myself and probably would have hurt myself physically in the aftermath. Allah didn't want me to feel the raw reality of meeting her and then have death yank her away right before my eyes. And on that note, all I could say was *Subhanallah* (Allah is Perfect, Glory be to Him), *Alhamdulillah* (All praises belong to Allah alone), *Allahuakbar* (Allah is the Greatest), and *La Ilaha Illa'llah* (None has the right to be worshipped except Allah).

* * *

Momma couldn't wait to tuck her grandbabies in bed. My twin daughters, Ayeesha and Zahra, were born on June 3, 2016. They were the products of my brief marriage to Hafiz, a distant family friend who later expressed interest in marrying me. In line with Islamic principles, Papa joined us in marriage immediately, but his family's heavy interference destroyed our marriage. It lasted for four years.

"I can't wait to chase them around the house," Momma would say, blushing infectiously. Samira had been trying for a child for over fourteen years, enduring six failed in vitro fertilizations (IVFs) and counting. It saddened me that my girls' chance of tasting a grandparent's love firsthand was cut off. I could tell by their interactions through video calls that their bond was intense. Death made it impossible for the girls to tease or anger *Moin* physically. For them, she remained the *Moin* that they would never meet.

Indeed, history has a brutal way of repeating itself. Like my girls, I too never met my grandparents on either side of the aisle. I had no firsthand memories of them. My paternal grandparents had perished before I was born. I was a baby when my maternal grandparents died. I admired my friends and their grandparents. I could only imagine what it was like to run into your grandparents' arms if you were beefing with your parents. My friend, Amaiyah, would always cause trouble at school and run to her grandparents' house for protection. I had to face my parents directly whenever I did something terrible. That grandparent bridge was missing, and it made me sick.

Momma always brought up my grandparents in conversations to help me piece things together. I questioned her about who they were and what they did for a living. I was saddened to learn that my maternal grandmother struggled immensely to make ends meet and was often sick. From what I knew, *Moin* Rokia was often hospitalized for stomach pain. She was later diagnosed with a massive bloodsucking intestinal worm that had already destroyed her organs, leading to her death. I was told she died young and never had the chance to see her children grow up. She had seven children, Momma being the second.

I also knew that my maternal grandfather was extraordinary because he consciously defied the socially prescribed notion that education was not right for girls. He sent all his twenty-one children to school, both boys and girls. He did this at a time when girls' education was strictly forbidden and considered an uncorrectable taboo by most diehard Merrivylle traditionalists.

Everyone had the same opportunity—call him the *most daring equal opportunity campaigner*. I was also told that my paternal grandfather was a great hunter and farmer who did everything he could to safeguard and sustain his family's health and happiness. He also had supernatural powers to transform himself into mighty creatures, such as lions, cheetahs, and so forth.

In general, I knew my grandparents were excellent role models on both sides of the family. I knew they would have given me so much love and joy even though I didn't meet them. I can't help but think of all the good memories I could have made with them. Luckily for my three-year-old twin daughters, there were images of Momma that they saw and cherished.

Ayeesha often screamed, "*Moin!*" whenever she saw Momma's picture anchored on my computer screen. I never saw photos of my grandparents. And if someone were to present one to me today, my first reaction would be, "Who's this person?" Whenever I think of them, I force myself to accept that their purpose on earth was fulfilled, which was why I didn't get a chance to meet them.

* * *

I touched down in the country of lights, life, and love. The country of sunflowers and pink peach trees. The country of laughing valleys and smiling rivers. Merrivylle was all that. It was a windy, wide-awake country situated in the heart of blushing pine trees. I could feel the joy. I was thrilled to be back after nearly eight years of absence from its soil. The air outside was steamy. I made my way through the arrival terminal, cautiously wheeling my six heavy suitcases and three overly stuffed carry-on valises while watching Ayeesha and Zahra. If nothing else, this was their first time flying and their very first time visiting the land of their mother's birth. I saw joy mixed with surprise on their faces.

While they were eager to interact physically with all the uncles and aunties they had seen through video chats, they were taken aback by the drastic change in scenery. Zinc-roofed, one-level brick houses replaced the multi-level skyscrapers they were used to seeing. Narrow two-way roads replaced the eight-lane I-95 highway. Trains and ventilated buses were replaced by rickety cabs and vans. The cultural shock was real, and the girls responded sharply.

They were glued to me, refusing to blend in with my family. Unlike Ayeesha, it took Zahra nearly four weeks to fully adjust. Ayeesha only needed two weeks to experiment with the neighborhood's chickens and ducks.

She fed the chickens with raw rice. "Mommy, let's go find the chickens," was the invitation I got every morning. She was amazed to see live chickens. Before this, her only experience with chickens was on Kid's YouTube or ABC Mouse, where she learned about farm animals.

"Mommy, the snails are crawling!" Zahra screamed on seeing live snails at a community market. This also was her reaction when she saw sheep, cows, goats, live crabs, only to mention a few. Of the two, Zahra was the most traumatized and would often throw a chaotic tantrum on coming face-to-face with live animals. She nearly fainted after spotting a live goat in the marketplace and later seeing roasted goat head and legs on display for sale. "Mommy! Isn't this the goat we just saw, standing on his legs?!"

Like her sister, Zahra would gradually immerse herself into this new culture and become familiar with its unique practices. Both girls learned to interact with new members of their maternal family. They learned their new home's feel, sounds, and smells, eventually creating their identities to blend further with their host land. Samira was crowned the youngest *Moin* (grandma), a task she took on with exceeding humility. "Small *Moin*," they called her.

* * *

As we approached the airport's chief exit, Omar hugged me. Samira appeared from my right. She hugged and kissed me and turned to hug the kids. The duo began counseling me as though they had it all planned, reminding me of life's brevity while searching my eyes for droplets.

"Every soul shall die," Omar began, looking sternly at me. "No soul shall be alive perpetually, and no soul shall die before its appointed time. Even death shall taste its handiwork at some point. Death shall die, just like all of us," he paused, searching Samira's face for backup comments. She didn't notice him. Her head was bowed.

Omar went on, "Don't even think about crying. We passed that stage long ago. Our Momma needs only one thing from us: prayers backed by unlimited good deeds. Let's pray for her. Her pains are over now. Her years of battle with fragile health are over now. May her Creator be pleased with her gentle soul and grant her paradise."

I saw Omar's lips move but heard nothing. I was standing motionless. Eyes fixed on the exact spot I had last seen Momma alive nearly eight years ago. I stared deeply into the spot and noticed an image of her reappear. She was in her favorite sky-blue floral dress, head veiled in a long white turban headscarf. She looked at me and looked away. Her sleek, silky brown skin glowed wildly against the rays of the fluorescent bulbs. Her eyes sparkled in their sockets. I rubbed my eyes as though to clear them, only to reopen them to see Momma standing in the same spot. This time, she wore a slight frown.

* * *

On the night of my departure from Merrivylle, we barely had any sleep. Everyone was nervous and afraid of being torn apart by distance. Regardless of Papa's nagging fear, we loved being together, being each other's rock. My trip to *Saboudou* took me far away from this stalwart crew of cheerleaders I had always known.

At 2:30 a.m. that morning, I rolled the suitcases outside our condo's narrow entrance but couldn't find our cab driver. Without a vehicle, we were compelled to walk the killer half mile distance up the main street to access public transport. I panicked, not for myself or my travel time, but Momma. She was visibly shaking, had lost massive weight, and struggled to stand still. Worst of all, we lived in a crabhole in a neighborhood way off the main motor road. I loaded a suitcase on my head. Samira took on the other. We sandwiched Momma, each person holding on tight to one of her arms while supporting the luggage on our heads with our left arms. We walked up the road at a snail's pace, barely making it through. We were soon blinded by

the headlights of an oncoming vehicle. I waved it down in hopes of nego-
tiating a new deal. "Are you Samira?" the driver asked as he rolled down
his windshield.

"Yes," Samira responded, peeping through the driver's side to ensure she
could identify the vehicle's operator. "Ah! Hassan. Is that you?" she asked.
"Yes, Samira. Please get in. I am so sorry for being late. I am not too familiar
with this area."

GPS devices or Google Maps were nonexistent in Merrivylle at the
time. Cab drivers, among other public transport operators, relied solely on
their mental map of the city. Paper maps were of no use as many commer-
cial drivers were unlettered. At the time, young boys were allowed to decide between going to school and being a handyman. Some had the chance
of being exposed to education. However, they dropped out after failing to
complete the A- or O-Levels. It was a diverse industry of semi-lettered
and unlettered actors, with the latter outweighing the former. So a paper
map detailing the direction to every street in the area was of no use, anyway.
Some drivers had an innate sense of direction. They used their brains to
navigate the city and were good at it. They explored the unknowns, walked
roads never taken, and thrived. Not even the old-school compass would
work for these drivers.

*　*　*

As Hassan loaded the suitcases into the trunk, I asked Samira if she knew
what she was doing. The gray hair, maroon eyebrows, and silver lashes of
Hassan bothered me.

"Is this the driver you negotiated with?"

"Of course! That's Hassan. What's the matter?" she asked.

"He looks so different."

"We don't have time for that. Let's go. Hassan isn't a ghost or some
reincarnation," she responded, looking furious. "Zaynab recommended him,

and I trust her recommendation. Shelve your fear, and let's get Momma off her feet." Okay, I got it. Samira was nervous. We all were, but I didn't want to put us in harm's way by jumping in the car of a half human. Samira dodged my hard looks, refusing to acknowledge the fear in my eyes, much less entertain my frowning.

Check-in was in progress as we pulled into the airport's lone parking lot. I grabbed a cart, loaded the suitcases, and wheeled them through the narrow entrance to hold a spot in the queue before dashing back outside. Once again, Samira and I sandwiched Momma between us and made our way inside. It was too late for last-minute chitchat. Momma and Samira anchored in a corner. There were no seats, not even a pillar to lean against. Samira positioned her body to provide support for Momma. She looked fragile but held on tight to see me fly, not knowing what lay ahead.

I returned after dropping off my suitcases, but boarding was announced. I hugged Momma tightly, refusing to let go. As I was about to cry, she said, "It breeds negativity."

"No matter what the outcome of this separation might be, Allah knows our hearts are pure." Looking at my stained face, she added, "Don't cry." She rubbed one hand across my face while rolling the other through my tightly braided micro cornrows. I rolled back my dams as I hugged and kissed her. I turned to Samira and said, "Please take good care of her. I will be back soon, *InshaAllah* (God willing)." I hugged Samira but failed to look her directly in the eyes. Her eyes were filled with tears. Seeing the tears in Samira's eyes would have compromised my decision to follow Momma's advice. Momma then said, "We are only being separated by distance, not in spirit. We will forever remain together."

"Do you see that little spot over there?" I asked, directing Momma and Samira to an opening behind the immigration officer's cubicle. "I will go through immigration but reappear there for my final goodbyes before heading upstairs. "No problem. We will wait for you," Momma said, readjusting herself as she leaned on Samira. "But don't be too long," she cautioned. "Remember, I have an 8:00 a.m. appointment with my doctor. Besides my legs can no longer support me in this position."

We were lucky to have identified a specialist to follow Momma for her illness. He was a prominent university professor, well abreast of trends in his medical specialty. He was excited to add Momma to the long list of clients he rendered incredible medical services to over the years. Until then, Momma had been seen by general practitioners who only used her as a case study but did little to suppress or manage her symptoms.

I hugged Momma before heading for passport control. As promised, I reappeared in the spot, waving and crying. Momma's voice came through, "Tears are not the right way to say goodbye."

"It's hard to keep them in," I said.

"We understand. It's never easy to say goodbye. But don't cry; it shall be well. We shall see you someday. Let's always pray for Allah's mercy in granting us good health and longevity," Momma stressed, fighting back her tears.

This journey wasn't one of my usual trips across the sub-region or a mini-vacay across the continent. It was a journey into the unknown, across the deep red sea. A journey that required so much effort (passports processing, visa application process, interviews, joggling in between airfares for the best) to see it through.

My sub-regional trips only required a bus or van ticket that cost roughly twenty dollars. However, the journey on this day required lots and lots of financial, emotional, and physical investments. No wonder overseas trips were always treated with particular sentiments among our people. Not everyone got so lucky to see its successful end, and most of those who were fortunate enough to see themselves with a green book stamped with a visa only imagined themselves walking on puffs of clouds.

As I walked through the glass door leading to the second floor, I cried inside and outside. I didn't know that was my last human contact with my rare mother.

* * *

While driving home that night, I cried but kept my tears within me - eventually flooding and flushing out my soul with sultry water. "Momma, where are you?" Momma, why aren't you here to welcome your grandbabies?" In a rhetorical tone, I asked, "What could I have done to save her life? Where did I get it wrong?" The questions went on and on and on.

At home, I sniffed Momma's mattress to sense her presence. Caressed her endless list of medical reports, lab results, and pharmacy slips. Massaged the remaining pills in each bottle. In her clothes, I wrapped myself up. Then I heard a female voice, partly similar to Momma's, saying, "Get some rest." I was surprised to find no one in the living room. I wondered, "Who would have said that?" I was in awe. Everyone was asleep. It was 5:00 a.m. "Could this be her?"

PART TEN

How I Wish

I divorced the denial when I saw Momma's grave the next morning. It left me with nothing. I greeted and began talking to her:

"Salaam, Momma. Wow.... So, this is actually how our reunion turned out. We are both in different worlds: human and spirit worlds. Momma, do both worlds ever meet? I guess you responded that they are very parallel, never to mingle. But how about dreams? Don't they blend in visions or nightmares when we, mortals, are subconscious? Ugh. I wish there were a bridge connecting both worlds. Since you departed our world, I haven't even seen or spoken with you. Samira told me it's because I won't stop crying. Is that true?

"I know your answer is a partial yes, trying so hard to make me feel good. Right? But I don't want that this time. I know I messed up and want to fix it, Momma. Please let me see you. Please appear to me. Don't worry. I won't be scared. I may be scared of other ghosts, but not you, Momma, because you are and will forever be my Momma and me, your little golden girl. Your new neighbors are pretty young, though. To your left is a twenty-four-year-old lady, and to your right is a twenty-year-old lady. They are lucky to have you, a sweet, cheerful sixty-year-old woman lying in the middle."

I turned to the graves on either side of hers and greeted: "Salaam, my fellow Muslims. May Allah be pleased with your souls and grant you all *Al Jannat.*" Turning to Momma's grave, I said, "Momma, forgive me for not returning soon enough to see you. Here I am, after seven years, feeling empty. I hate home. I hate myself. I know you missed me unmeasurably. I did too. Here are your grandbabies."

I asked the girls to greet *Moin.* They looked puzzled but obliged. Ayeesha climbed atop the grave and submerged herself in the shimmery marbles that covered Momma. "It feels like a swimming pool," she said, inviting Zahra to jump in. Together, they played on the grave while I sat there, conversing with my invisible Momma.

"I know you are sitting here with me, seeing and hearing me and even speaking back to me. I may not be able to respond directly to you, which may affect the flow of our conversation, but I'm here to ask for your forgiveness and to pray for Allah's bounteous mercies on your gentle soul. May He be pleased with you, forgive your worldly shortcomings, widen and lighten up your new home."

Throughout my twelve-week stay, I spent hours by Momma's grave daily, speaking my heart out, knowing and believing she was up and listening to me. I was inspired by the story of two orphan toddlers who visited their mom's grave daily for food. According to a legend, a four-year-old held her one-year-old baby brother's hand and led him to their mother's grave every morning and evening. The younger child was still breastfeeding when their mom passed away. As the story went, whenever they arrived at the cemetery, their mom's grave opened up; she was awakened and would feed her baby for hours before the toddler took her sibling back to the village. This back and forth went on for months until the cemetery guardian became aware of the situation one night. An announcement was made at the village masjid, and residents volunteered to provide food and shelter for the orphans.

Inspired by this story, and fueled by my unwavering faith in Allah's Mighty power, I sat by Momma's grave, talking solo for hours every day. I spent long hours on Mondays, Thursdays, and Fridays because, according to Omar, deceased Muslims were awakened on such days. "Momma would be up and will see you on these days," he said. So, I knew that she was there, even though I couldn't see or hear her. I did all these save wailing at her grave. I sealed up and booked my tears in my heart. I would cry, internally only, melting my heart. Samira had succeeded in scaring me: crying drives a mother's spirit farther away from her children.

* * *

We held a prayer service for Momma on Sunday, July 21. It all began at 4:00 a.m. Multiple women gathered in mini circles of eight to slice and blend mixed vegetables while dicing fresh cow meat. There were five extra-large pots mounted on gas-powered stoves. In each saucepan, raw ingredients boiled leisurely, emitting a pleasant aroma that quickly invaded the entire neighborhood. Several workstations were up and running by 6:00 a.m. Teams of women divided brown rice into tons of retail bags for easy distribution. Mini goodie bags were filled with boxes of stuffed waffle biscuits, sacks of mildly ripe dates, and mini packs of powdered milk. Over 300 mourners had gathered the night before to pray and give charity in memory of my amazingly superb mother, and by 7:00 a.m., a pot of steamed beans adorned with meat and vegetables stew had been devoured by them.

Momma's prayer service was graced by seven imams. They offered *du'aa'* (supplications), comforting and reminding the living of the brevity of life. "What are you taking along [with you to your grave]?" one imam asked, somewhat rhetorically. "Death," he said, "instantly strips us of everything save our deeds (good or bad). That's the only thing we take to our grave." May our good deeds always outweigh our shortcomings.

*   *   *

Four weeks after my return to Cherry City, Momma visited me for the first time. She was convinced and believed in my determination to seal my tears. She looked her usual self, like how she looked before being knocked down by the sickness. She was with two of her favorite siblings, Saleem and Djènnè. Suddenly she left for an unknown location, hoping to be back soon. She never returned as early as expected. Omar and I went looking for her. Then my phone rang. It was Momma:

"Hey Manatou, you remember the phone I told you about?"

"Which phone?"

"The iPhone I always told you about."

"Ah, ok…"

"I just saw a similar phone with someone here. I want you to buy me that phone. I still need it."

"Of course, I remember. I will get it for you this weekend. But where are you?"

She never responded, and we never found her. I woke up the next morning, went into a T-Mobile store, and purchased the phone. I then gave it to charity, praying for Allah to remit the blessings to her in her grave.

PART ELEVEN
A Powerless Death

I trained myself to intentionally believe in my Momma's presence in everything I did and everywhere I went—this was my idea of easing my pain. Our old folks said, "Our loved ones do not leave us, even in death," for "death is not as dreadful" after all. It was a brief period of complete unconsciousness, a short but deep dream from which its victims were awakened, mostly upon arriving in their graves. The longer it took a dead to reach their final resting place, the longer their sleep. This is why Islam encouraged us to bury the dead as quickly as possible. All they needed was quick access to their grave, and death would be powerless against them.

I knew Momma was awake eternally, and death could no longer harm her. She peacefully transitioned on Monday night, June 10, 2019, and was laid to rest in the early afternoon of Tuesday, June 11, 2019.

I knew this was not enough to make saying goodbye to Momma any easier. However, it strengthened me to reflect on the joyful moments we shared. We were best friends and fans of each other. Without her, my life would never be what it was, but then again, Allah always knew and did what was best. Who were we to doubt His plans?

* * *

I finally understood what mourners meant by "you will learn to live through it," though I vehemently resented everyone who said this to me during Momma's seventh-day burial ritual in Pittsburgh. I hated the cliché that "time heals all wounds. With time, you will be fine." I resented relatives who tried encouraging me not to cling to grief too tightly. "It will get used to you, and you will find it difficult to break free from it. Breathe, believe, and let go." I also frowned at friends who told me, "Time will heal you." I considered it sarcastic since most of those saying this still had their mothers around. Mine was gone. How could they even imagine my pain? How could they understand that healing took time because grief must be embraced first and foremost? How could they understand that time had little to offer regarding healing from layered pain? They were clueless.

Having accepted her death, remembering Momma became easy. However, missing her still gave me persistent heartache. I wrapped myself in her scarf each night, wide awake in bed when the world was buried in deep sleep. Samira stepped up and played key roles in my life. The kids knew and loved her. She checked on me multiple times daily, spending long hours on the phone. In case of a connection problem on her end, she worried about being unable to speak with me. She was an active listener, always willing to let me vent. She knew that she would never take Momma's place in my heart, but she still made healing attainable for me, despite the triangular shape of my heart with an empty spot in its center. The upper part of my heart had a permanent dent that no one would ever fill. The right side was overwhelmed with tender memories of Momma; the left side had never recovered from her death; it died along with her.

PART TWELVE

The New Me

Five years later the gut-wrenching pain of losing Momma still ran deep. It didn't just go away, though, with time, it mellowed to a dull, perpetual ache—but even with that, I was regularly exposed to new waves of grief.

I found solace in memories of Momma, replaying those fond moments we shared and smiling at the thought of her calling me multiple play names, such as "Golden Girl," which was my favorite. My mind was now in survival mode. I no longer hated myself for doing so little to protect Momma from death (as though I had any such power); being in denial and feeling guilty were all parts of grief's tricky strategy to keep me glued to the nothingness inside me. Granted, life went on, but I was sure there would never be a full stop to me breaking down whenever I thought of Momma. Once grief was inside you, it settled in and popped up at will.

There were no prescriptions or shortcuts to grieving. In my case, I longed for a reset button. I was never prepared for the sporadic explosions of heartache that consumed me at inappropriate times. Once, I saw a photo of a coworker and her mother hugging each other. I dashed out to cry in my car, in gulping sobs. After overhearing someone talk about their mother,

I rushed out of the office to cry in my car. Reading an obituary on social media brought tears to my eyes. I related to it. A scene in a movie when a mother died was enough to trigger the droplets in my eyes. I was also jealous whenever I saw others hang out with their mothers while traveling, shopping, and even gossiping. Long story short, any mother-daughter moment made me sad. At the same time, these moments reminded me of how strong a relationship this was and how lucky I had been to share those decades of my life with mine.

I was furious when a friend blasted her mother for not waking up early to prepare the kids for school. "You simply hate that you are lucky," I told her. I regretted that I never had a photo of Momma and me together. The ones we had were all damaged in the tribal war, and over the years, we were consumed by Momma's on-and-off health crisis so much that it never occurred to me that I needed a photo for a day like today. I had started planning an elaborate surprise sixtieth birthday party featuring multiple photoshoots with Momma—but she had spent her birthday, June 8, on a sickbed, ruining this plan. She passed away just two days after turning sixty.

* * *

Grief was a strict teacher, reminding me of critical life lessons I previously took for granted. I was now opened to greater understanding and compassion for myself and those around me. The way I looked at life had changed forever. I was worried about the possibility of squandering it while pursuing the world's pleasures. Momma's passing taught me that it was okay to enjoy life. Yet it was prudent to be mindful of your limits. Excessive enjoyment easily made us forget about the hereafter, which was a sign of a *wasted life*, as Papa would say. I worried that I might have gone too far in my desire to enjoy the world. I regretted not heeding Papa's advice not to become attached to earthly pleasures. He enjoined me to desist from the pleasures of the earth, but I didn't listen: "They are trials. They will be your enemies if you are so attached to them."

* * *

Momma's death taught me that the worldly life I was so obsessed with would vanish one day. "So why not ensure my hereafter is peaceful by seeking Allah's blessings and enlightenment? After all, my deeds on earth are the only things that will follow me into my grave. Not the expensive gold necklaces, outfits, diamond jewelry, etc. Just my deeds—good and bad. But! I want to ensure that my good deeds outweigh the other," I advised myself. And trust me, it was final.

The love affair I had with wigs, weaves, or other hair extensions was over. There were a lot of wigs and weaves in my closet - some I hadn't worn, and some that cost me more than $1,000. I piled them in a trash bag, ready to part ways with them forever. At first, I entertained the thought of donating them to those who would use them, but that was also unreligious—it was no different from me wearing them myself. So I threw them away, which was the right thing to do.

I resolved never to delay salat again. Before Momma's passing, I was quite a delinquent prayer, often offering salat an hour or two after its appointed time. Not that I didn't know this was religiously unacceptable. I did! Besides, Momma constantly reminded me of the importance of offering salat at the right time. "Once you hear the Azan, drop everything and worship Allah." Yet I could not faithfully observe these established Islamic principles due to my love for the world. In short, I was a Muslim in theory.

* * *

I began fasting, a religious must-do I didn't pay much attention to until now. I further adjusted my wardrobe to truly reinforce modesty. At least this time, it was a decision by me, of me, and for me. I veiled my head, setting off my journey as a hijab enthusiast, which was a huge responsibility to take on, but I was ready. I didn't care if this meant that friends would neglect me. It wasn't about what they wanted or thought my life should be. That was mine to decide and implement. I took serious exception when a male relative said, "You've been wrapping your head a lot lately. What are you up to? Whatever it is, make sure you don't end up veiling completely."

"And how does any of that impact your life?" I asked furiously.

"Veils are meant for older women. A young, beautiful woman like yourself shouldn't be concealing your beauty," he responded audaciously.

"And which part of that concerns you? The veil? My age? Or me being a woman?" I was angry. "I don't live my life to please you or anyone else. What pleases me is what I do."

From then on, I never entertained curious questions from people in my family about my life as a hijabi. I cut off every link to this unwanted social pressure. I didn't even care who was looking at me or talking about me each time I stepped out in my modest attire. Momma always encouraged me to be bold and proud of my religious identity and display it wherever and whenever. "It's always good to be known by your religion. Let your faith define you," she said, though I never heeded her advice at the time. However, deciding to veil my head was the best decision I ever made.

When Momma was alive, I never bothered controlling my fear and anxiety. I was susceptible, often pouting. My greatest fear was rejection. I felt defeated whenever I was rejected for whatever reason or by whomever. It took Momma several days to restore me to my usual self after being hit by a rejection notice or letter. I was emotionally fragile and did nothing about it besides being aware that this issue existed. However, Momma's passing taught me to be resilient and to have thick skin. It made me stronger, wiser.

I understood that rejections didn't mean the end of the world. They also didn't mean I wasn't good enough. They only confirmed that specific routes weren't paved or built for me to travel or that particular doors weren't mine to bash into. *Shrug it off and get moving. Keep exploring until you can find yours!* I finally accepted that what was destined for me would always come smiling at me—no matter what or how long it took. I accepted that no amount of rejection or denial was good enough to make me give up. I would keep knocking. As Momma would say, "If it is your door, it will open. In case it doesn't, consider it a redirection. Believe in you." I now believe in myself.

I lost my most significant connection to life when Momma died. Her death taught me never to take anything seriously. I lost expensive pieces of jewelry, and it felt like nothing had happened. Who cares about losing costly jewels? Momma's death strengthened me to tackle other life losses with resistance, resolve, and resoluteness—nothing else mattered.

*   *   *

Momma would have been sixty-five this year. She would have been here with me in Cherry City. By now, we would have had her daycare up and running because my lackadaisical babysitter was neglectful, and it hurt my heart that I had no choice but to deal with this lazy caregiver. I dropped off the kids each morning, along with a baby bag stuffed with a change of clothes, extra diapers, wipes, snacks, etc. Yet I picked up my kids drenched. I *had* to deal with it because it was affordable care, and Momma wasn't around to save me the headache. Nadiatou's strategic location in the neighborhood made her the go-to for nearly every immigrant mother looking for alternative childcare. Being an immigrant from Merrivylle further polished her competitive edge—making her the *perfect babysitter* in the area.

The high cost of daycare forced us to seek out low-cost babysitters, whose service, however, was terrible. In Cherry City, preschoolers' regular daycare fees started at $300 a week. That was $1,200 per month, compared to $300 or $400 spent on babysitters monthly. Besides, the $1,200 average monthly daycare fee was way beyond the operating budgets of most immigrant moms making nine to fourteen dollars an hour. On average, babysitters charged fifteen dollars per child per day. Nadiatou, my babysitter, charged fifteen dollars per child (ages five to ten) and twenty dollars per toddler (ages four and below). And with nearly twenty children making the rounds at her house daily, one could safely say this woman was bagging nearly $2,000 in babysitting fees daily.

"Yet she refuses to care for our kids properly," I told Momma one afternoon, voice trembling. "Granted, toddlers will get messy when they play. But if our kids consistently need changing when we pick them up or are always soaked in their urine, that's a problem."

"Manatou, stop. Please don't cry. You will make me cry if you do," Momma went on, tears drenching her blouse as we chatted through WhatsApp video call. "If your babysitter can't take care of the basics, that's a sign that she's just too lazy to meet your child's needs," she said. Momma cried so hard that I forgot about my pain. I was now consoling her.

That's just how emotionally connected we were. She wholeheartedly reciprocated the love: Momma cried whenever I did, she smiled whenever I did. It was that contagious. Now that she was gone, I had daily moments when I felt mired in sadness. To those in my condition and anyone just joining this motherless club, I am deeply and profoundly sorry. I feel your pain. I know and understand exactly how this goes down. It is awful, but you are not alone, and there is no right or wrong way to deal with such a substantial loss. Sit on the couch and cry when you need to. Get up and go freshen up in the shower. Take a long, therapeutic bath. Then find that peculiar thing, place, or person where the memories of your departed loved one were anchored. Mine was Samira. She had Momma's face, cheeks, nose, eyes, hair, body, and height. She was Momma's replica, and I ran to her to feel a close semblance of Momma. I also listened to Momma's favorite songs—"Badénya" by Sekouba Bambino, "Moûsso" by Salif Keita, only to mention a few—to relive some of my most cherished moments with her.

* * *

I encouraged Samira to reactivate Momma's M.T.N. cell number. I didn't want us to bury all of her memories along with her. I had previously asked her to disconnect the line but later thought that that would dishonor Momma's legacy. She was dead but never gone. We distributed her clothes among relatives and took some as inheritances. I took her two favorite dresses that she wore almost every time we video-chatted. When I picked those two, I was asked why I didn't take the nicest and most beautiful ones. Who cares about beauty? I just wanted a living memory of her, and those two dresses served that purpose for me.

I wore them often to offer salat and thank Allah, asking Him to enrich Momma's grave with blessings, lights, and peace. I also found solace in fulfilling her wishes by helping others, especially the needy. I established an informal public charity dedicated to carrying on her legacy of respect for humanity, being kind to others.

Momma's death taught me that living and enjoying life while remaining religiously obedient were two sides of the same coin. It wasn't necessary to give up one in order to gain the other, as was my experience over the years. Throughout my life, I believed that the only way to be religiously obedient was to sever ties with all things worldly, as Papa had said. Yet it dawned on me that it was possible to live life while repairing my relationship and maintaining close ties with my Maker. I no longer took the doomsday rhetoric for granted but never allowed it to cloud my ability to rest easy and enjoy life.

By the fifth anniversary of Momma's passing, I had learned to live again, though my life remained sadder. I started frequenting the malls, going to movies, and strolling through neighborhood recreation parks. Being alone was a breeding ground for my internal demons. So I stepped out often and held lengthy phone conversations. I had handled Momma's medical bills for nineteen years but wholeheartedly embraced victimhood, though doing so was unreligious. Islam taught us that no soul perished before its appointed time. Though I wish I had seen her before all this, her passing in my absence was the will of Allah, and I had to repent and seek Allah's forgiveness for being in denial for too long.

Welcome to the new Manatou Lahai.

Glossary of French, Arabic, and Mandingo Words Used Throughout the Text

Badénya: brotherhood, sisterhood

Signônya: neighborliness

Les Médiateurs: The Mediators

Amour: love

Moin: grandma

Mousso: women

Tête-à-tête: head-to-head

Dunya: world

Tiatoulou: peanut oil

Al Jannat: heaven

Jahim: hell

Baramorsama: goodies for the family

Ayat Kursi: a Qur'anic verse for Allah's protection

Tounghan: journeying in unknown territories

Koniaka: an ethnic group of West Africa

Lagaré: princess

N'dianamösso: city of my beloved

Damasa: djinn

Soumbarafeen: a typical Mandingo seasoning

Lafidi: dry rice

Tö: cassava and plantain dough

Nanjee: clear, pepper soup

Tiajee: *peanut soup*

Farafina: Africa

Tantie: an aunt, a maternal or paternal relative

Milton Keynes UK
Ingram Content Group UK Ltd.
UKHW012250290324
440241UK00004B/276